"There are rules tonight, Alessia, and you will play by them."

"Will I?" she asked.

She wasn't sure why she was goading him. Maybe because it was the only way in all the world she could feel as if she had some power. Or maybe it was because if she wasn't trying to goad him she would be longing for him. And the longing was just unacceptable.

A smile curved his lips and she couldn't help but wonder if he needed this too. This edge of hostility, the bite of anger between them.

Although why Matteo would need anything to hold her at a distance when he'd already made his feelings quite clear was a mystery to her.

"Yes, my darling wife, you will."

He put his hand on her chin, drawing close to her, his heat making her shiver deep inside. It brought her right back to the hotel.

SICILY'S CORRETTI DYNASTY

The more powerful the family...the darker the secrets!

Mills & Boon® Modern™ Romance introduces the Correttis:

Sicily's most scandalous family!

Behind the closed doors of their opulent *palazzo*, ruthless desire and the lethal Corretti charm are alive and well.

We invite you to step over the threshold
and enter the Correttis' dark and dazzling world...

The Empire
They're young, rich, and notoriously handsome—the Correttis'
legendary exploits regularly feature in Sicily's tabloid pages!

The Scandal
But how long can their reputations withstand the glaring heat
of the spotlight before the family's secrets are exposed?

The Legacy
Once nearly destroyed by the secrets cloaking their thirst for
power, the new generation of Correttis are riding high again—
and no disgrace or scandal will stand in their way...

Sicily's Corretti Dynasty

A LEGACY OF SECRETS
Carol Marinelli

AN INVITATION TO SIN
Sarah Morgan

A SHADOW OF GUILT
Abby Green

AN INHERITANCE OF SHAME
Kate Hewitt

A WHISPER OF DISGRACE
Sharon Kendrick

A FAÇADE TO SHATTER
Lynn Raye Harris

A SCANDAL IN THE HEADLINES
Caitlin Crews

A HUNGER FOR THE FORBIDDEN
Maisey Yates

8 volumes to collect—you won't want to miss out!

A HUNGER FOR
THE FORBIDDEN

BY
MAISEY YATES

MILLS & BOON

First published in Great Britain 2013
by Mills & Boon, an imprint of Harlequin (UK) Limited.
Harlequin (UK) Limited, Eton House, 18-24 Paradise Road,
Richmond, Surrey TW9 1SR

© Harlequin Books S.A. 2013

Special thanks and acknowledgement are given to Maisey Yates
for her contribution to *Sicily's Corretti Dynasty* series

ISBN: 978 0 263 23596 8

Maisey Yates knew she wanted to be a writer even before she knew what it was she wanted to write.

At her very first job she was fortunate enough to meet her own tall, dark and handsome hero, who happened to be her boss, and promptly married him and started a family. It wasn't until she was pregnant with her second child that she found her very first Harlequin Mills & Boon® book in a local thrift store—by the time she'd reached the happily ever after she had fallen in love. She devoured as many as she could get her hands on after that, and knew that these were the books she wanted to write!

She started submitting and nearly two years later, while pregnant with her third child, she received 'The Call' from her editor. At the age of twenty-three she sold her first manuscript, and was very glad that the good news didn't send her into labour!

She still can't quite believe she's blessed enough to see her name on not just *any* book, but on her favourite books.

Maisey lives with her supportive, handsome, wonderful, diaper-changing husband and three small children across the street from her parents and the home she grew up in, in the wilds of southern Oregon. She enjoys the contrast of living in a place where you might wake up to find a bear on your back porch, then walk into the home office to write stories that take place in exotic, urban locales.

Other titles by Maisey Yates:

HIS RING IS NOT ENOUGH
THE COUPLE WHO FOOLED THE WORLD
HEIR TO A DARK INHERITANCE
  (Secret Heirs of Powerful Men)
HEIR TO A DESERT LEGACY
  (Secret Heirs of Powerful Men)

To the fabulous editors at the M&B office.
You push me to be better and to take risks.
And you make my job fun.
Thank you.

CHAPTER ONE

ALESSIA BATTAGLIA ADJUSTED her veil, the whisper-thin fabric skimming over the delicate skin of her neck. Like a lover's kiss. Soft. Gentle.

She closed her eyes, and she could feel it.

Hot, warm lips on her bare flesh. A firm, masculine hand at her waist.

She opened her eyes again and bent down, adjusting the delicate buckles on her white satin heels.

Her lover's hands on her ankle, removing her high heels. Leaving her naked in front of him, naked before a man for the first time. But there was no time for nerves. There was nothing more than the heat between them. Years of fantasy, years of longing.

Alessia swallowed and took the bouquet of bloodred roses from the chair they were resting on. She looked down at the blossoms, some of them bruised by the way she'd laid them down.

Brushing her fingertips over the crushed velvet petals brought another wave of memory. A wave of sensation.

Her lover's mouth at her breast, her fingers woven through his thick dark hair.

"Alessia?"

Her head snapped up and she saw her wedding coordinator standing in the doorway, one hand covering her headset.

"Yes?"

"It's time."

Alessia nodded, and headed toward the doorway, her shoes loud on the marble floor of the basilica. She exited the room that had been set aside for her to get ready in, and entered the vast foyer. It was empty now, all of the guests in the sanctuary, waiting for the ceremony.

She let out a long breath, the sound loud in the empty, high-ceilinged room. Then she started her walk toward the sanctuary, past pillars inlaid with gold and stones. She stopped for a moment, hoping to find some comfort, some peace, in the biblical scenes depicted on the walls.

Her eyes fell to a detailed painting of a garden. Of Eve handing Adam the apple.

"Please. Just one night."

"Only one, cara mia*?"*

"That's all I have to give."

A searing kiss, like nothing she'd ever experienced before. Better than any fantasy.

Her breath caught and she turned away from the painting, continuing on, continuing to the small antechamber outside of the sanctuary.

Her father was there, his suit crisp and pressed. Antonioni Battaglia looked every inch the respectable citizen everyone knew he was not. And the wedding, so formal, so traditional, was another statement of his power. Power that he longed to increase, with the Corretti fortune and status.

That desire was the reason she was here.

"You are very much like your mother."

She wondered if there was any truth to the words, or if it was just the right thing to say. Tenderness was something her father had never seemed capable of.

"Thank you," she said, looking down at her bouquet.

"This is what's right for the family."

She knew it was. Knew that it was the key to ensuring

that her brothers and sisters were cared for. And that was, after all, what she'd done since her mother died in childbirth. Pietro, Giana, Marco and Eva were the brightest lights in her existence, and she would do, had done, whatever she could to ensure they had the best life possible.

And still, regret settled on her like a cloak, and memory clouded the present. Memories of her lover. His hands, his body, his passion.

If only her lover, and the man waiting behind the doors to the sanctuary, waiting to marry her, were the same.

"I know," she said, fighting against the desolation inside of her. The emptiness.

The double doors parted, revealing an impossibly long aisle. The music changed, everyone turned to look at her— all twelve hundred guests, who had come to watch the union of the Battaglia family and their much-hated rivals, the Correttis.

She held her head up, trying to breathe. The bodice of her dress threatened to choke her. The lace, which formed a high collar, and sleeves that ended in a point over her hands, was heavy and scratched against her skin. The yards of fabric clung to her, heat making her feel light-headed.

It was a beautiful dress, but it was too fussy for her. Too heavy. But the dress wasn't about her. The wedding wasn't about her.

Her father followed her into the sanctuary but didn't take her arm. He had given her away when he'd signed his agreement with the late Salvatore Corretti. He didn't need to do it again. He didn't move to take a seat, either, rather he prowled around the back of the pews, up the side of the church, his steps parallel to hers. That was Antonioni Battaglia all over. Watching proceedings, ensuring all went well. Watching her. Making sure she did as she was told.

A drop of sweat rolled down her back and another flash of memory hit her hard.

His sweat-slicked skin beneath her fingertips. Her nails digging into his shoulders. Her thighs wrapped around lean, masculine hips...

She blinked and looked up at Alessandro. Her groom. The man to whom she was about to make her vows.

God forgive me.

Had she not been holding the roses, she would have crossed herself.

And then she felt him. As though he had reached out and put his hands on her.

She looked at the Corretti side, and her heart stopped for a moment. Matteo.

Her lover. Her groom's enemy.

Matteo was arresting as ever, with the power to draw the breath from her lungs. Tall and broad, his physique outlined to perfection by his custom-made suit. Olive skin and square jaw. Lips that delivered pleasure in beautiful and torturous ways.

But this man standing in the pews was not the man who'd shared her bed that night a month ago. He was different. Rage, dark and bottomless, burned from his eyes, his jaw tight. She had thought, had almost hoped, that he wouldn't care about her being promised to Alessandro. That a night of passion with her would be like a night with any other woman.

Yes, that thought had hurt, but it had been better than this. Better than him looking at her like he hated her.

She could remember those dark eyes meeting hers with a different kind of fire. Lust. Need. A bleak desperation that had echoed inside of her. And she could remember them clouded by desire, his expression pained as she'd touched him, tasted him.

She looked to Alessandro but she could still feel Matteo watching her. And she had to look back. She always had to look at Matteo Corretti. For as long as she could remember, she'd been drawn to him.

And for one night, she'd had him.

Now…now she would never have him again.

Her steps faltered, her high heel turning sideways beneath her. She stumbled, caught herself, her eyes locking with Matteo's again.

Dio, it was hot. Her dress was suffocating her now. The veil too heavy on her head, the lace at her throat threatening to choke her.

She stopped walking, the war within her threatening to tear her to pieces.

Matteo Corretti thought he would gag on his anger. Watching her walk toward Alessandro, his cousin, his rival in business and now, because of this, his enemy.

Watching Alessia Battaglia make her way to Alessandro, to bind herself to him.

She was Matteo's. His lover. His woman. The most beautiful woman he had ever seen in his life. It wasn't simply the smooth perfection of her golden skin, not just the exquisite cheekbones and full, rose-colored lips. It was something that existed beneath her skin, a vitality and passion that had, by turns, fascinated and confused him.

Her every laugh, every smile, every mundane action, was filled with more life, more joy, than his most memorable moments. It was why, from the first time he'd sneaked a look at her as a boy, he had been transfixed.

Far from the monster he'd been made to believe the Battaglias were, she had been an angel in his eyes.

But he had never touched her. Never breached the unspoken command issued by his father and grandfather. Because she was a Battaglia and he a Corretti, the bad blood between them going back more than fifty years. He had been forbidden from even speaking to her and as a boy he had only violated that order once.

And now, when Salvatore had thought it might benefit him, now she was being traded to Alessandro like cattle. He tightened his hands into fists, anger, anger like he hadn't felt in more than thirteen years, curling in his gut. The kind of rage he normally kept packed in ice was roaring through him. He feared it might explode, and he knew what happened when it did.

He could not be held responsible for what he might do if he had to watch Alessandro touch Alessia. Kiss her.

And then Alessia froze in place, her big, dark eyes darting from Alessandro, and back to him. Those eyes. Those eyes were always in his dreams.

Her hand dropped to her side, and then she released her hold on her bouquet of roses, the sound of them hitting the stone floor loud in the sudden silence of the room.

Then she turned, gripping the front of her heavy lace skirt, and ran back down the aisle. The white fabric billowed around her as she ran. She only looked behind her once. Wide, frightened eyes meeting his.

"Alessia!" He couldn't stop himself. Her name burst from his lips, and his body burst from its position in the pews. And he was running, too. "Alessia!"

The roar of the congregation drowned out his words. But still he ran. People were standing now, filing into the aisle, blocking his path. The faces of the crowd were a blur, he wasn't aware of who he touched, who he moved out of his way, in his pursuit of the bride.

When he finally burst through the exterior doors of the basilica, Alessia was getting into the backseat of the limo that was waiting to carry her and her groom away after the ceremony, trying to get her massive skirt and train into the vehicle with her. When she saw him, everything in her face changed. A hope in her eyes that grabbed him deep in his chest and twisted his heart. Hard.

"Matteo."

"What are you doing, Alessia?"

"I have to go," she said, her eyes focused behind him now, fearful. Fearful of her father, he knew. He was gripped then by a sudden need to erase her fears. To keep her from ever needing to be afraid again.

"Where?" he asked, his voice rough.

"The airport. Meet me."

"Alessia…"

"Matteo, please. I'll wait." She shut the door to the limo and the car pulled out of the parking lot, just as her father exited the church.

"You!" Antonioni turned on him. "What have you done?"

And Alessandro appeared behind him, his eyes blazing with fury. "Yes, cousin, what have you done?"

Alessia's hands shook as she handed the cash to the woman at the clothing shop. She'd never been permitted to go into a store like this. Her father thought this sort of place, with mass-produced garments, was common. Not for a Battaglia. But the jeans, T-shirt and trainers she'd found suited her purpose because they were common. Because any woman would wear them. Because a Battaglia would not. As if the Battaglias had the money to put on the show they did. Her father borrowed what he had to in order to maintain the fiction that their power was as infinite as it ever was. His position as Minister for the Trade and Housing department might net him a certain amount of power, power that was easily and happily manipulated, but it didn't keep the same flow of money that had come from her grandfather's rather more seedy organization.

The shopgirl looked at her curiously, and Alessia knew

why. A shivering bride, sans groom, in a small tourist shop still wearing her gown and veil was a strange sight indeed.

"May I use the changing room?" she asked once her items were paid for.

She felt slightly sick using her father's money to escape, sicker still over the way she'd gotten it. She must have been quite the sight in the bank, in her wedding gown, demanding a cash advance against a card with her father's name on it.

"I'm a Battaglia," she'd said, employing all the self-importance she'd ever heard come from Antonioni. "Of course it's all right for me to access my family money."

Cash was essential, because she knew better than to leave a paper trail. Having a family who had, rather famously, been on the wrong side of the law was helpful in that regard at least. As had her lifelong observation of how utter confidence could get you things you shouldn't be allowed to have. The money in her purse being a prime example.

"Of course," the cashier said.

Alessia scurried into the changing room and started tugging off the gown, the hideous, suffocating gown. The one chosen by her father because it was so traditional. The virgin bride in white.

If he only knew.

She contorted her arm behind her and tugged at the tab of the zip, stepping out of the dress, punching the crinoline down and stepping out of the pile of fabric. She slipped the jeans on and tugged the stretchy black top over her head.

She emerged from the room a moment later, using the rubber bands she'd purchased to restrain her long, thick hair. Then she slipped on the trainers, ruing her lack of socks for a moment, then straightened.

And she breathed. Feeling more like herself again. Like

Alessia. "Thank you," she said to the cashier. "Keep the dress. Sell it if you like."

She dashed out of the store and onto the busy streets, finally able to breathe. Finally.

She'd ditched the limo at the bank, offering the driver a generous tip for his part in the getaway. It only took her a moment to flag down a cab.

She slid in the back, clutching her bag to her chest. "Aeroporto di Catania, *per favore.*"

"Naturalmente."

Matteo hadn't lingered at the basilica. Instead, he'd side-stepped his cousin's furious questions and gotten into his sports car, roaring out of the parking lot and heading in the direction of the airport without giving it any thought.

His heart was pounding hard, adrenaline pouring through him.

He felt beyond himself today. Out of control in a way he never allowed.

In a way he rarely allowed, at least. There had been a few breaks in his infamous control, and all of them were tied to Alessia. And they provided a window into just what he could become if the hideous cold that lived in him met with passionate flame.

She was his weakness. A weakness he should never have allowed and one he should certainly never allow again.

Dark eyes clashing with his in a mirror hanging behind the bar. Eyes he would recognize anywhere.

He turned sharply and saw her, the breath pulled from his lungs.

He set his drink down on the bar and walked across the crowded room, away from his colleagues.

"Alessia." He addressed her directly for the first time in thirteen years.

"Matteo." His name sounded so sweet on her lips.

It had been a month since their night together in New York City, a chance encounter, he'd imagined. He wondered now.

A whole month and he could still taste her skin on his tongue, could still feel the soft curves of her breasts resting in his palms. Could still hear her broken sighs of need as they took each other to the height of pleasure.

And he had not wanted another woman since.

They barely made it into his hotel room, they were far too desperate for each other. He slammed the door, locking it with shaking fingers, pressing her body against the wall. Her dress was long, with a generous slit up the side, revealing her toned, tan legs.

He wrapped his fingers around her thigh and tugged her leg up around his hip, settling the hardness of his erection against her softness.

It wasn't enough. It would never be enough.

Matteo stopped at a red light, impatience tearing at him. Need, need like he had only known once before, was like a beast inside him, devouring, roaring.

Finally, she was naked, her bare breasts pressing hard against his chest. He had to have her. His entire body trembling with lust.

"Ready for me, cara mia?"

"Always for you."

He slid inside of her body, so tight, much more so than he'd expected, than he'd ever experienced. She cried out softly, the bite of her nails in his flesh not due to pleasure now.

A virgin.

His. Only his.

Except she had not been his. It had been a lie. The next morning, Alessia was gone. And when he'd returned to Sicily, she'd been there.

He'd been invited to a family party but he had not realized that all branches of the Corretti family would be
present. Had not realized it was an engagement party. For
Alessandro and Alessia. A party to celebrate the end of a
feud, the beginning of a partnership between the Battaglias
and the Correttis, a chance to revitalize the docklands in
Palermo and strengthen their family corporation.

"How long have you and Alessia been engaged?" he
asked, his eyes trained on her even as he posed the question to Alessandro.

*"For a while now. But we wanted to wait to make the
big announcement until all the details were finalized."*

"I see," he said. *"And when is the blessed event?"*

"One month. No point in waiting."

Some of the old rage burned through the desire that
had settled inside of him. She had been engaged to Alessandro when he'd taken her into his bed. She'd intended,
from the beginning, to marry another man the night she'd
given herself to him.

And he, he had been forced to watch her hang on his
cousin's arm for the past month while his blood boiled in
agony as he watched his biggest rival hold on to the one
thing he wanted more than his next breath. The one thing
he had always wanted, but never allowed himself to have.

He had craved violence watching the two of them together. Had longed to rip Alessandro's hands off her and
show him what happened when a man touched what belonged to him.

Even now, the thought sent a rising tide of nausea
through him.

What was it Alessia did to him? This wave of posses-
siveness, this current of passion that threatened to drown
him, it was not something that was a part of him. He was
a man who lived in his mind, a man who embraced logic
and fact, duty and honor.

When he did not, when he gave in to emotion, the danger was far too great. He was a Corretti, cut from the same cloth as his father and grandfather, a fabric woven together with greed, violence and a passion for acquiring more money, more power, than any one man could ever need.

Even with logic, with reason, he could and had justified actions that would horrify most men. He hated to think what might happen if he were unleashed without any hold on his control.

So he shunned passion, in all areas of life.

Except one.

He pulled his car off the road and slammed on his breaks, killing the engine, his knuckles burning from the hard grip he had on the steering wheel, his breath coming in short, harsh bursts.

This was not him. He didn't know himself with Alessia, and he never had.

And nothing good could come from it. He had spent his life trying to change the man he seemed destined to be. Trying to keep control, to move his life in a different direction than the one his father would have pushed him into.

Alessia compromised that. She tested it.

He ran his fingers through his hair, trying to catch his breath.

Then he turned the key over, the engine roaring to life again. And he turned the car around, heading away from the airport, away from the city.

He punched a button on his dashboard and connected himself to his PA.

"Lucia?"

"Si?"

"Hold my calls until further notice."

It had been three hours. No doubt the only reason her father and his men hadn't come tearing through the airport was that they would never have imagined she would do something so audacious as to run away completely.

Alessia shifted in the plastic chair and wiped her cheek again, even though her tears had dried. She had no more tears left to cry. It was all she'd done since she'd arrived.

And she'd done more since it had become clear Matteo wasn't coming.

And then she'd done more when she'd suddenly had to go into the bathroom and throw up in a public stall.

Then she'd stopped, just long enough to go into one of the airport shops and pick up the one thing she'd avoided buying for the past week.

She'd started crying again when the pregnancy test had resulted in two little pink, positive, yes-you're-having-a-baby lines.

Now she was wrung out. Sick. And completely alone.

Well, not completely alone. Not really. She was having a baby, after all.

The thought didn't comfort her so much as magnify the feeling of utter loneliness.

One thing was certain. There was no going back to Alessandro. No going back to her family. She was having the wrong man's baby. A man who clearly didn't want her.

But he did once.

That thought made her furious, defiant. Yes, he had. More than once, which was likely how the pregnancy had happened. Because there had been protection during their times in bed, but they'd also showered together in the early hours of the morning and then…then neither of them had been able to think, or spare the time.

A voice came over the loudspeaker, the last call for her flight out to New York.

She stood up, picked up her purse, the only thing she

had with her, the only thing she had to her name, and handed her ticket to the man at the counter.

"Going to New York?" he asked, verifying.

She took a deep breath. "Yes."

CHAPTER TWO

He'd never even opened the emails she'd been sending him. She knew, because she'd set them up so that they would send her a receipt when the addressee opened her message, but she'd never gotten one.

He didn't answer her calls, either. Not the calls to his office, not the calls to his mobile phone, not the calls to the Palazzolo Corretti, or to his personal estate outside Palermo.

Matteo Corretti was doing an exceptional job of ignoring her, and he had been for weeks now while she'd been holed up in her friend Carolina's apartment. Carolina, the friend who had talked her into a New York bachelorette party in the first place. Which, all things considered, meant she sort of owed Alessia since that bachelorette party was the source of both her problems, and her pregnancy.

No, that wasn't fair. It was her fault. Well, a lot of it was. The rest was Matteo Corretti's. Master of disguise and phone-call-avoider extraordinaire.

She wished she didn't need him but she didn't know what else to do. She was so tired. So sad, all the time. Her father wouldn't take her calls, either, her siblings, the most precious people in her life were forbidden from speaking to her. That, more than anything, was threatening to burn a hole in her soul. She felt adrift without them around her. They'd kept her going for most of her life, given her a sense of purpose, of strength and responsibility. Without them she just felt like she was floundering.

She'd had one option, of course. To terminate the pregnancy and return home. Beg her father and Alessandro for forgiveness. But she hadn't been able to face that. She'd lost so much in her life already and as confused as she was about the baby, about what it would mean for her, as terrified as she was, she couldn't face losing the tiny life inside of her.

But she would run out of money soon. Then she would be alone and penniless while Matteo Corretti spent more of his fortune on sports cars and high-rise hotels.

She wasn't going to allow it anymore. Not when she'd already decided that if he didn't want to be a part of their baby's life he would have to come tell her to her face. He would have to stand before her and denounce their child, verbally, not simply by ignoring emails and messages. He would have to make that denouncement a physical action.

Yes, she'd made the wrong decision to sleep with him without telling him about Alessandro. But it didn't give him the right to deny their child. Their child had nothing to do with her stupidity. He or she was the only innocent party in the situation.

She looked down at the screen on her phone. She had her Twitter account all set up and ready to help her contact every news outlet in the area.

She took a breath and started typing.

@theobserver @NYTnews @HBpress I'm about to make an important announcement re Matteo Corretti & the wedding scandal. Luxe Hotel on 3rd.

Then she stepped out of the back of the cab and walked up to the front steps of Matteo's world-renowned hotel, where he was rumored to be in residence, though no one would confirm it, and waited.

The sidewalks were crowded, people pushing past other people, walking with their heads down, no one sparing her a glance. Until the news crews started showing up.

First there was one, then another, and another. Some from outlets she hadn't personally included in her tweet. The small crowd drew stares, and some passersby started lingering to see what was happening.

There was no denying that she was big news. The assumption had been that she'd run off with Matteo but nothing could be further from the truth. And she was about to give the media a big dose of truth.

It didn't take long for them to catch the attention of the people inside the hotel, which had been a key part of her plan.

A sharply dressed man walked out of the front of the hotel, his expression wary. "Is there something I can help you with?"

She turned to him. "I'm just making a quick announcement. If you want to go get Matteo, that might help."

"Mr. Corretti is not in residence."

"That's like saying someone isn't At Home in a Regency novel, isn't it? He's here, but he doesn't want anyone to know it."

The reporters were watching the exchange with rapt attention, and the flash on one of the cameras started going, followed by the others.

"Mr. Corretti is not—"

She whirled around to face him again. "Fine, then if Mr. Corretti is truly not in residence you can stand out here and listen to what I have to say and relay it to your boss when you deliver dinner to the room he is not in residence in."

She turned back to the reporters, and suddenly, the official press release she'd spent hours memorizing last night seemed to shatter in her brain, making it impossible to piece back together, impossible to make sense of it.

She swallowed hard, looking at the skyline, her vision filled with concrete, glass and steel. The noise from the cars was deafening, the motion of the traffic in front of her making her head swim. "I know that the wedding has been much talked about. And that Matteo chasing me out of the church has been the headline. Well, there's more to the story."

Flashes blinded her, tape recorders shoved into her face, questions started to drown out her voice. She felt weak, shaky, and she wondered, not for the first time, if she was completely insane.

Her life in Sicily had been quiet, domestic, one surrounded by her family, one so insular that she'd been dependent upon imagination to make it bearable, a belief of something bigger looming in her future. And as a result, she had a tendency to romanticize the grand gesture in her mind. To think that somehow, no matter how bleak the situation seemed, she could fix it. That, in the end, she would make it perfect and manage to find her happy ending.

She'd done it on the night of her bachelorette party. New York was so different than the tiny village she'd been raised in. So much bigger, faster. Just being there had seemed like a dream and so when she'd been confronted with Matteo it had seemed an easy, logical thing to approach him, to follow the path their mutual attraction had led them down. It was a prime example of her putting more stock in fantasy, in the belief in happy endings, over her common sense.

This was another.

But no matter how well planned this was, she hadn't realized how she would feel, standing there with everyone watching her. She wasn't the kind of woman who was used to having all eyes on her, her aborted wedding being the exception.

"I'm pregnant, and Matteo Corretti is the father of my baby." It slipped out, bald and true, and not at all what she'd been planning to say. At least she didn't think it was.

"Mr. Corretti—" the employee was speaking into his phone now, his complexion pallid "—you need to come out here."

She released a breath she hadn't realized she'd been holding.

"When is the baby due?"

"Are you certain he's the father?"

"When did you discover you were pregnant?"

The questions were coming rapid-fire now, but she didn't need to answer them because this was never about the press. This was about getting his attention. This was about forcing a confrontation that he seemed content to avoid.

"I'll answer more questions when Matteo comes to make his statement."

"Did the two of you leave the wedding together, or are you estranged? Has he denied paternity?" one of the reporters asked.

"I…"

"What the hell is going on?"

Alessia turned and her heart caught in her throat, making it impossible to breathe. Matteo. It felt like an eternity since she'd seen him, since he'd kissed her, put his hands on her skin. An eternity.

She ached with the need to run to him, to hold on to him, use him as an anchor. In her fantasies, he had long been her knight in shining armor, a simplistic vision of a man who had saved her from a hideous fate.

But in the years since, things had changed. Become more complex, more real. He was her lover now. The father of her child. The man she had lied to. The man who had left her sitting alone in an airport, crying and clutching a positive pregnancy test.

For a moment, the longing for those simple, sun-drenched days in Sicily, when he had been nothing more than an idealized savior, was so sharp and sweet she ached.

"Mr. Corretti, is this why you broke up the wedding?"

"I didn't break up anyone's wedding," he said, his tone dark.

"No, I ran out of the wedding," she said.

"And is what why I broke up the wedding?" he asked, addressing the reporter, stormy eyes never once looking at her.

"The baby," the reporter said.

Matteo froze, his face turning to stone. "The baby." Color drained from his face, but he remained stoic, only the change in his complexion a clue as to the shock that he felt.

He didn't know. She felt the impact of that reality like a physical blow. He hadn't even listened to a single message. Hadn't opened any emails, even before she'd started tagging them to let her know when he opened them.

"Is there more than one?" This from another reporter.

"Of course not," Matteo said, his words smooth, his eyes cold like granite. "Only this one."

He came to stand beside her, his gaze still avoiding hers. He put his arm around her waist, the sudden contact like touching an open flame, heat streaking through her veins. How did he manage to affect her this way still? After all he'd done to her? After the way he'd treated her?

"Do you have a statement?"

"Not at this point," he bit out. "But when the details for the wedding are finalized, we will be in touch."

He tightened his hold on her waist and turned them both around, away from the reporters, leading her up the steps and into the hotel. She felt very much like she was being led into the lion's den.

"What are you doing?" she asked, wishing he would move away from her, wishing he would stop touching her.

"Taking you away from the circus you created. I have no desire to discuss this with an audience."

If he wasn't so angry with her, she might think it was a good idea. But Matteo Corretti's rage was like ice-cold water in a black sea. Fathomless, with the great threat of pulling her beneath the waves.

His hold tightened with each step they took toward the hotel, and her stomach started to feel more and more unsettled until, when they passed through the revolving door and into the hotel lobby, she was afraid she might vomit on the high-gloss marble floors.

A charming photo to go with the headlines.

He released her the moment they were fully inside. "What the hell is the meaning of this?" he asked, rounding on her as his staff milled around very carefully not watching.

"Should we go somewhere more private?" she asked. Suddenly she felt like she'd rather brave his rage than put on a show. She was too tired for that. Too vulnerable. Bringing the press in was never about drawing attention to herself, it was about getting information to Matteo that he couldn't ignore. Giving the man no excuse to say he didn't know.

"Says the woman who called a bloody press conference?"

"You didn't answer my calls. Or return my messages. And I'm pretty sure now that you didn't even listen to any of them."

"I have been away," he said.

"Well, that's hardly my fault that you chose this moment to go on sabbatical. And I had no way of knowing."

He was looking at her like she'd grown an extra head. "Take me to your suite," she said.

"I'm not in the mood, Alessia."

"Neither am I!" she shot back. "I want to talk."

"It's just that last time we were in this hotel, talking was very much not on the agenda."

Her face heated, searing prickles dotting her skin. "No. That's very true. Which is how we find ourselves in this current situation."

"Communication seems to be something we don't do well with," he said. "Our lack of talking last time we were here together certainly caused some issues."

"But I want to talk now," she said, crossing her arms beneath her breasts.

He cocked his head to the side, dark eyes trained on her now with a focus he'd withheld until that moment. "You aren't afraid of me."

"No."

"A mistake, some might say, *cara mia*."

"Is that so?"

"You won't like me when I'm angry."

"You turn green and split your pants?"

"Perhaps taking this somewhere private is the best idea," he said, wrapping his fingers around her arm, just above her elbow, and directing her toward the elevator.

He pushed the up button and they both waited. She felt like she was hovering in a dream, but she dug her fingernails into her palms, and her surroundings didn't melt away. It was real. All of this.

The elevator doors slid open and they both stepped inside. And as soon as they were closed into the lift, he rounded on her.

"You're pregnant?" His words were flat in the quiet of the elevator.

"Yes. I tried to tell you in a less public way, but it's been two months and you've been very hard to get ahold of."

"Not an accident."

"Oh, no, I know. It was far too purposeful to be accidental. You never even opened my emails."

"I blocked your address after you sent the first few."

"Uh," she said, unable to make a more eloquent sound.

"I see it offends you."

"Yes. It does offend me. Didn't it occur to you that I might have something important to tell you?"

"I didn't care," he said.

The elevator stopped at the top floor and the doors slid open. "Is there a point in me going any further, then? Or should I just go back to my friend Carolina's apartment and start a baby registry?"

"You are not leaving."

"But you just said you didn't care."

"I didn't care until I found out you were carrying my child."

She was both struck, and pleased, by his certainty that the child was his. She wouldn't have really blamed him if he'd questioned her at least once. She'd lied about her engagement to Alessandro. By omission, but still. She knew she wasn't blameless in the whole fiasco.

"What did you think I was trying to contact you for? To beg you to take me back? To beg you for more sex? Because that's what we shared that night, that's all we shared." The lie was an acid burn on her tongue. "I would hardly have burned my pride to the ground for the sake of another orgasm."

"Is that true? You would hardly be the first person to do it."

"If you mean you, I'm sure it cost you to take a Battaglia to your bed. Must have been some epic dry spell."

"And not worth the price in the end, I think."

His words were designed to peel skin from bone, and they did their job. "I would say the same."

"I can see now why you ran from the wedding."

A wave of confusion hit her, and it took her a moment to realize that she hadn't told him the order in which the events had occurred. Wedding abandonment, then pregnancy test, but before she could correct him he pressed on.

"And how conveniently you've played it, too. Alessandro would, of course, know it wasn't his child as you never slept with him. I hope you're pleased with the way all of this unfolded because you have managed to ensure that you are still able to marry a Corretti, in spite of our little mistake. Good insurance for your family since, thanks to your abandonment, the deal between our family and yours has gone to hell."

"You think I planned this? You aren't even serious about marrying me, are you?"

"There is no other choice. You announced your pregnancy to the whole world."

"I had to tell you."

"And if I had chosen not to be a part of the baby's life?"

"I was going to make you tell me that to my face."

He regarded her closely. "Strange to think I ever imagined you to be soft, Alessia."

"I'm a Battaglia. I've never had the luxury of being soft."

"Clearly not." He looked at her, long and hard. "This makes sense, Alessia." His tone was all business now. Maddeningly sure and decisive. "It will put to rest rumors of bad blood, unite the families."

"You didn't seem to care about that before."

"That was before the baby. The baby changes everything."

Because he wanted to make a family? The idea, so silly and hopeful, bloomed inside of her. It was her blessing and curse that she always found the kernel of hope in any situation. It was the thing that got her through. The thing that had helped her survive the loss of her mother, the cold detachment from her father, the time spent caring for her siblings when other girls her age were out dating, having lives, fulfilling dreams.

She'd created her own. Locked them inside of her. Nurtured them.

"I… It does?" she asked, the words a whisper.

"Of course," he said, dark eyes blazing. "My child will be a Corretti. On that, there can be no compromise."

CHAPTER THREE

MATTEO'S OWN WORDS echoed in his head.

My child will be a Corretti. On that there can be no compromise.

It was true. No child of his would be raised a Battaglia. Their family feud was not simply a business matter. The Battaglias had set out to destroy his grandfather, and had they succeeded they would have wiped out the line entirely.

It was the hurt on her face that surprised him, and more than that, his response to it.

Damn Alessia Battaglia and those dark, soulful eyes. Eyes that had led him to ruin on more than one occasion.

"Because you won't allow your child to carry my name?" she asked.

"That's right."

"And what of my role in raising my child?"

"You will, of course, be present."

"And what else? Because more than mere presence is required to raise a child."

"Nannies are also required, in my experience."

"In your experience raising children, or being raised?"

"Being raised. I'm supremely responsible in my sexual encounters so I've never been in this situation before."

"Supremely responsible?" she asked, cheeks flushing a gorgeous shade of rose that reminded him of the blooms in his Sicilian palazzo. "Is that what you call having sex with your cousin's fiancée with no condom?"

Her words, so stark and angry, shocked him. Alessia had always seemed fragile to him. Sweet. But tangling with her today was forcing him to recognize that she was also a woman capable of supreme ruthlessness if the situation required it.

Something he had to reluctantly respect.

"I didn't know you were engaged to be married, as you withheld the information from me. As to the other issue, that has never happened to me before."

"So you say."

"It has not," he said.

"Well, it's not like you were overly conscious of it at the time."

Shame cracked over his insides like a whip. He had thought himself immune to shame at this point. He was wrong. "I knew. After."

"You remembered and you still didn't think to contact me?"

"I did not think it possible." The thought hadn't occurred to him because he'd been too wrapped up in simply trying to avoid her. Alessia was bad for him, a conclusion he'd come to years ago and reaffirmed the day he'd decided not to go after her.

And now he was bound to her. Bound to a woman who dug down far too deep inside of him. Who disturbed his grasp on his control. He could not afford the interruption. Could not afford to take the chance that he might lose his grip.

"Why, because only other people have the kind of sex that makes babies?"

"Do you always say what comes to your mind?"

"No. I never do. I never speak or act impulsively, I only think about it. It's just you that seems to bring it out."

"Aren't I lucky?" Her admission gripped him, held him. That there was something about him that brought about a change in her...that the thing between them didn't only shatter his well-ordered existence but hers, too, was not a comfort. Not in the least.

"Clearly, neither of us are in possession of much luck, Alessia."

"Clearly," she said.

"There is no way I will let my child be a bastard. I've seen what happens to bastards. You can ask my cousin Angelo about that." A cousin who was becoming quite the problem. It was part of why Matteo had come to New York, why he was making his way back into circulation. In his absence, Angelo had gone and bought himself a hefty amount of shares for Corretti Enterprises and at this very moment he was sitting in Matteo's office, the new head of Corretti Hotels. He'd been about to go back and make the other man pay. Wrench the power right back from him.

Now, it seemed there was a more pressing matter.

"So, you're doing this to save face?"

"For what other reason? Do you want our child to be sneered at? Disgraced? The product of an illicit affair between two of Sicily's great warring families?"

"No."

Matteo tried not to read the emotion in her dark eyes, tried not to let them pull him in. Always, from the moment he'd seen her, he'd been fascinated. A young girl with flowers tangled in her dark hair, running around the garden of her father's home, a smile on her lips. He could remember her dancing in the grass in her bare feet, while her siblings played around her.

And he had been transfixed. Amazed by this girl who, from all he had been told, should have been visibly evil in some way. But she was a light. She held a brightness and joy like he had never seen. Watching it, being close enough to touch it, helped him pretend it was something he could feel, too.

She made him not so afraid of feeling.

She'd had a hold on him from day one. She was a sorceress. There was no other explanation. Her grip on him defied logic, defied every defense he'd built inside of himself.

And no matter how hard he tried, he could read her. Easily. She was hurt. He had hurt her.

"What is it?" he asked.

She looked away. "What do you mean?"

"Why are you hurt?"

"You've just told me how unlucky we both are that I'm pregnant—was I supposed to look happy?"

"Don't tell me you're pleased about this. Unless it was your plan."

"How could I have...planned this? That doesn't make any sense."

He pushed his fingers through his hair and turned away from her. "I know. *Che cavolo*, Alessia, I know that." He turned back to her.

"I just wanted to tell you about the baby."

He felt like he was drowning, like every breath was suffocating him. A baby. She was having his baby. And he was just about the last man on earth who should ever be a father. He should walk away. But he couldn't.

"And this was the only way?"

Her eyes glittered with rage. "You know damn well it was!"

He did. He'd avoided her every attempt at contacting him. Had let his anger fuel the need for distance between them. Had let the very existence of the emotion serve as a reminder. And he had come back frozen again. So he'd thought. Because now Alessia was here again, pushing against that control.

"Why didn't you meet me at the airport?" she asked, her words a whisper.

"Why didn't I meet you?" he asked, his teeth gritted. "You expected me to chase after you like a dog? If you think you can bring me to heel that easily, Alessia, you are a fool."

"And if you think I'm trying to you're an idiot, Matteo Corretti. I don't want you on a leash."

"Well, you damn well have me on one!" he said, shouting for the first time, his tenuous grip on his control slipping. "What am I to do after your public display? Deny my child? Send you off to raise it on your own? Highly unlikely."

"How can we marry each other? We don't love each other. We barely like each other right now!"

"Is that so bad? You were prepared to marry Alessandro, after all. Better the devil you know. And we both know you know me much better than you knew him."

"Stop it," she said, the catch in her voice sending a hot slash of guilt through his chest. Why he was compelled to lash out at her, he wasn't sure.

Except that nothing with Alessia was ever simple. Nothing was ever straightforward. Nothing was ever neat or controlled.

It has to be.

"It's true, though, isn't it, Alessia?" he asked, his entire body tense now. He knew for a fact he was the first man to be with her, and something in him burned to know that he had been the only man. That Alessandro had never touched her as he had. "You were never with him. Not like you were with me."

The idea of his cousin's hands on her... A wave of red hazed his vision, the need for violence gripping his throat, shaking him.

He swallowed hard, battled back the rage, fought against

images that were always so close to the surface when Alessia was around. A memory he had to hold on to, no matter how much he might wish for it to disappear.

Blood. Streaked up to his elbows, the skin on his knuckles broken. A beast inside of him unleashed. And Alessia's attackers on the ground, unmoving.

He blinked and banished the memory. It shouldn't linger as it did. It was but one moment of violence in a lifetime of it. And yet, it had been different. It had been an act born of passion, outside of his control, outside of rational thought.

"Tell me," he ground out.

"Do you honestly think I would sleep with Alessandro after what happened?"

"You were going to. You were prepared to marry him. To share his bed."

She nodded wordlessly. "Yes. I was."

"And then you found out about the baby."

"No," she said, her voice a whisper.

"What, then?"

"Then I saw you."

"Guilt?"

"We were in a church."

"Understandable."

"Why didn't you meet me?" she asked again, her words holding a wealth of pain.

"Because," he said, visions of blood washing through his brain again, a reminder of what happened when he let his passions have control, "I got everything I wanted from you that night. Sex. That was all I ever wanted from you, darling."

She drew back as though he'd struck her. "Is that why you've always watched me?"

"I'll admit, I had a bit of an obsession with your body, but you know you had one with mine."

"I liked you," she said, her words hard, shaky. "But you never came near me after—"

"There is no need to dredge up the past," he said, not wanting to hear her speak of that day. He didn't want to hear her side of it. How horrifying it must have been for a fourteen-year-old girl to see such violence. To see what he was capable of.

Yet, she had never looked at him with the shock, the horror, he'd deserved. There was a way she looked at him, as though she saw something in him no one else did. Something good. And he craved that feeling. It was one reason he'd taken her up on her invitation that night at the hotel bar.

Too late, he realized that he was not in control of their encounter that time, either. No, Alessia stole the control. Always.

No more, he told himself again.

Alessia swallowed back tears. This wasn't going how she'd thought it would. Now she wasn't sure what she thought. No, she knew. Part of her, this stupid, girlish, optimistic part of her, had imagined Matteo's eyes would soften, that he would smile. Touch her stomach. Take joy in the fact that they had created a life together.

And then they would live happily ever after.

She was such a fool. But Matteo had long been the knight in shining armor of her fantasies. And so in her mind he could do no wrong.

She'd always felt like she'd known him. Like she'd understood the serious, dark-eyed young man she'd caught watching her when she was in Palermo. Who had crept up to the wall around her house when he was visiting his grandmother and stood there while she'd played in the garden. Always looking like he wanted to join in, like he wanted to play, but wouldn't allow himself to.

And then...and then when she'd needed him most, he'd

been there. Saved her from…she hardly even knew what horror he'd saved her from. Thank God she hadn't had to find out exactly what those two men had intended to use her for. Matteo had been there. As always. And he had protected her, shielded her.

That was why, when she'd seen him in New York, it had been easy, natural, to kiss him. To ask him to make love to her.

But after that he hadn't come to save her.

She looked at him now, at those dark eyes, hollow, his face like stone. And he seemed like a stranger. She wondered how she could have been so wrong all this time.

"I don't want to dredge up the past. But I want to know that the future won't be miserable."

"If you preferred Alessandro, you should have married him while you had him at the altar with a priest standing by. Now you belong to me, the choice has been taken. So you should make the best of it."

"Stop being such an ass!"

Now he looked shocked, which, she felt, was a bit of an accomplishment. "You want me to tell you how happy I am? You want me to lie?"

"No," she said, her stomach tightening painfully. "But stop…stop trying to hurt me."

He swore, an ugly, crude word. "I am sorry, Alessia, it is not my intent."

The apology was about the most shocking event of the afternoon. "I…I know this is unexpected. Trust me, I know."

"When did you find out?" he asked.

"At the airport. So…if you had met me, you would have found out when I did."

"And what did you do after that?"

"I waited for you," she said. "And then I got on a plane

and came to New York. I have a friend here, the friend that hosted my little bachelorette party."

"Why did you come to New York?"

"Why not?" She made it sound casual, like it was almost accidental. But it wasn't. It had made her feel close to him, no matter where he might have been in the world, because it was the place she'd finally been with him the way she'd always dreamed of. "Why did you come to New York?"

"Possibly for the same reason you did," he said, his voice rough. It made her stomach twist, but she didn't want to ask him for clarification. Didn't want to hope that it had something to do with her.

She was too raw to take more of Matteo's insults. And she was even more afraid of his tenderness. That would make her crumble completely. She couldn't afford it, not now. Now she had to figure out what she was doing. What she wanted.

Could she really marry Matteo?

It was so close to her dearest fantasy. The one that had kept her awake long nights since she was a teenager. Matteo. Hers. Only hers. Such an innocent fantasy at first, and as she'd gotten older, one that had become filled with heat and passion, a longing for things she'd never experienced outside of her dreams.

"And if…" she said, hardly trusting herself to speak "… if we marry, my family will still benefit from the merger?"

"Your father will get his money. His piece of the Corretti empire, as agreed upon."

"You give it away so easily."

"Because my family still needs the docklands revitalization. And your father holds the key to that."

"And it will benefit Alessandro, too."

"Just as it would have benefitted me had he married you."

Those words, hearing that it would have benefitted him

for her to marry someone else, made her feel ill. "So a win all around for the Correttis, then?"

"I suppose it is," he said.

There was a ruthless glint in his eyes now. One she had never seen directed at her before. One she'd only seen on one other occasion.

"What if I say no?" she asked, because she had to know. She wasn't sure why she was exploring her options now. Maybe because she'd already blown everything up. Her father likely hated her.... Her siblings...they must be worried sick. And she wondered if anyone was caring for them properly.

Yes, the youngest, Eva, was fourteen now and the rest of them in their late teens, but still, she was the only person who nurtured them. The only person who ever had.

The life she'd always known, the life she'd clung to for the past twenty-seven years, was changed forever. And now she felt compelled in some ways to see how far she could push it.

"You won't say no," he said.

"I won't?"

"No. Because if you do, the Battaglias are as good as bankrupt. You will be cared for, of course our child will be, too. I'm not the kind of man who would abandon his responsibility in that way. But what of your siblings? Their care will not be my problem."

"And if I marry you?"

"They'll be family. And I take care of family."

A rush of joy and terror filled her in equal parts. Because in some ways, she was getting just what she wanted. Matteo. Forever.

But this wasn't the Matteo she'd woven fantasies around. This was the real Matteo. Dark. Bitter. Emotionless in a way she'd somehow never realized before.

He'd given her passion on their night together, but for

the most part, the lights had been off. She wondered now if, while his hands had moved over her body with such skill and heat, his eyes had been blank and cold. Like they were now.

She knew that what she was about to agree to wasn't the fantasy. But it was the best choice for her baby, the best choice for her family.

And more fool her, she wanted him. Still. All of those factors combined meant there was only ever one answer for her to give.

"Yes, Matteo. I'll marry you."

CHAPTER FOUR

THE HUSH IN the lobby of Matteo's plush Palermo hotel was thick, the lack of sound more pronounced and obvious than any scream could have been.

It was early in the day and employees were milling around, setting up for a wedding and mobilizing to sort out rooms and guests. As Matteo walked through, a wave of them parted, making room for him, making space. Good. He was in no mood to be confronted today. No mood for questions.

Bleached sunlight filtered through the windows, reflecting off a jewel-bright sea. A view most would find relaxing. For him, it did nothing but increase the knot of tension in his stomach. Homecoming, for him, would never be filled with a sense of comfort and belonging. For him, this setting had been the stage for violence, pain and shame that cut so deep it was a miracle he hadn't bled to death with it.

He gritted his teeth and pulled together every last ounce of control he could scrape up, cooling the anger that seemed to be on a low simmer in his blood constantly now.

He had a feeling, though, that the shock was due only in part to his presence, with a much larger part due to the woman who was trailing behind him.

He punched the up button for the elevator and the doors slid open. He looked at Alessia, who simply stood there, her hands clasped in front of her, dark eyes looking at everything but him.

"After you, *cara mia*," he said, putting his hand between the doors, keeping them from closing.

"You don't demand that a wife walk three paces behind you at all times?" she asked, her words soft, defiant.

"A woman is of very little use to me when she's behind me. Bent over in front of me is another matter, as you well know."

Her cheeks turned dark with color, and not all of it was from embarrassment. He'd made her angry, as he'd intended to do. He didn't know what it was about her that pushed him so. That made him say things like that.

That made him show anything beyond the unreadable mask he preferred to present to the world.

She was angry, but she didn't say another word. She simply stepped into the elevator, her eyes fixed to the digital readout on the wall. The doors slid closed behind them, and still she didn't look at him.

"If you brought me here to abuse me perhaps I should simply go back to my father's house and take my chances with him."

"That's what you call abuse? You didn't seem to find it so abhorrent the night you let me do it."

"But you weren't being a bastard that night. Had you approached me at the bar and used it as a pickup line I would have told you to go to hell."

"Would you have, Alessia?" he asked, anger, heat, firing in his blood. "Somehow I don't think that's true."

"No?"

"No." He turned to her, put his hand, palm flat, on the glossy marble wall behind her, drawing closer, drawing in the scent of her. *Dio.* Like lilac and sun. She was Spring standing before him, new life, new hope.

He pushed away from her, shut down the feeling.

"Shows what you know."

"I know a great deal about you."

"Stop with the you-know-me stuff. Just because we slept together—"

"You have a dimple on your right cheek. It doesn't show every time you smile, only when you're really, really smiling. You dance by yourself in the sun, you don't like to wear shoes. You've bandaged every scraped knee your brothers and sisters ever had. And whenever you see me, you can't help yourself, you have to stare. I know you, Alessia Battaglia, don't tell me otherwise."

"You knew me, Matteo. You knew a child. I'm not the same person now."

"Then how is it you ended up in my bed the night of your bachelorette party?"

Her eyes met his for the first time all morning, for the first time since his private plane had touched down in Sicily. "Because I wanted to make a choice, Matteo. Every other choice was being made for me. I wanted to…I wanted to at least make the choice about who my first lover should be."

"Haven't you had a lot of time to make that choice?"

"When? With all of my free time? I've spent my life making sure my brothers and sisters were cared for, really cared for, not just given the bare necessities by staff. I spent my life making sure they never bore the full brunt of my father's rage. I've spent my life being the perfect daughter, the hostess for his functions, standing and smiling next to him when he got reelected for a position that he abuses."

"Why?" he asked.

"Because of my siblings. Because no matter that my father is a tyrant, he is our father. We're Battaglias. I hoped… I've always hoped I could make that mean something good. That I could make sure my brothers and sisters learned to do the right things, learned to want the right things. If

I didn't make sure, they would only have my father as a guiding influence and I think we both know Antonioni Battaglia shouldn't be anyone's guiding influence."

"And what about you?"

"What about me?"

The elevator doors slid open and they stepped out into the empty hall on the top floor.

"You live your whole life for other people?"

She shook her head. "No. I live my life in the way that lets me sleep at night. Abandoning my brothers and sisters to our father would have hurt me. So it's not like I'm a martyr. I do it because I love them."

"But you ran out on the wedding."

She didn't say anything, she simply started walking down the hall, her heels clicking on the marble floor. He stood and watched her, his eyes drifting over her curves, over that gorgeous, heart-shaped backside, outlined so perfectly by her pencil skirt.

It looked like something from the Corretti clothing line. One thing he might have to thank his damn brother Luca for. But it was the only thing.

Especially since the rumor was that in his absence the other man was attempting to take Matteo's share in the Corretti family hotels. A complete mess since that bastard Angelo had his hands in it, as well.

A total mess. And one he should have anticipated. He'd dropped out of the dealings with Corretti Enterprises completely since the day of Alessia and Alessandro's aborted wedding. And the vultures had moved in. He should try to stop them, he knew that. And he could, frankly. He had his own fortune, his own power, independent of the Corretti machine, but at the moment, the most pressing issue was tied to the tall, willowy brunette who was currently sauntering in the wrong direction.

"The suite is this way," he said.

She stopped, turned sharply on her heel and started walking back toward him, past him and down the hall.

He nearly laughed at the haughty look on her face. In fact, he found he wanted to, but wasn't capable of it. It stuck in his throat, his control too tight to let it out.

He walked past her, to the door of the suite, and took a key card out of his wallet, tapping it against the reader. "My key opens all of them."

"Careful, *caro*, that sounds like a bad euphemism." She shot him a deadly look before entering the suite.

"So prickly, Alessia."

"I told you you didn't know me."

"Then help me get to know you."

"You first, Matteo."

He straightened. "I'm Matteo Corretti, oldest son of Benito Corretti. I'm sure you know all about him. My criminal father who died in a fire, locked in an endless rivalry with his brother, Carlo. You ought to know about him, too, as you were going to marry Carlo's son. I run the hotel arm of my family corporation, and I deal with my own privately owned line of boutique hotels, one of which you're standing in."

She crossed her arms and cocked her hip out to the side. "I think I read that in your online bio. And it's nothing I don't already know."

"That's all there is to know."

She didn't believe that. Not for a moment. She knew there was more to him than that. Knew it because she'd seen it. Seen his blind rage as he'd done everything in his power to protect her from a fate she didn't even like to imagine.

But he didn't speak of it. So neither did she.

"Tell me about you," he said.

"Alessia Battaglia, Pisces, oldest daughter of Antonioni. My father is a politician who does under-the-table dealings with organized-crime families. It's the thing that keeps him in power. But it doesn't make him rich. It's why he needs the Correttis." She returned his style of disclosure neatly, tartly.

"The Correttis are no longer in the organized-crime business. In that regard, my cousins, my brothers and I have done well, no matter our personal feelings for each other."

"You might not be criminals but you are rich. That's why you're so attractive. In my father's estimation at least."

"Attractive enough to trade us his daughter."

She nodded. She looked tired suddenly. Defeated. He didn't like that. He would rather have her spitting venom at him.

"You could walk away, Alessia," he said. "Even now you could. I cannot keep you here. Your father cannot hold you. You're twenty-seven. You have the freedom to do whatever you like. Hell, you could do it on my dime since I'll be supporting my child regardless of what you do."

He didn't know why he was saying it, why he was giving her the out. But part of him wished she would take it. Wished she would leave him alone, take her beauty, the temptation, the ache that seemed to lodge in his chest whenever she was around, with her. The danger she presented to the walls of protection he'd built around his life.

She didn't say anything. She didn't move. She was frozen to the spot, her lips parted slightly, her breath shallow, fast.

"Alessia, you have the freedom to walk out that door if you want. Right now."

He took a step toward her, compelled, driven by something he didn't understand. Didn't want to understand. The beast in him was roaring now and he wanted it to shut up. Wanted his control back.

He'd had a handle on it again. Had moved forward from

the events of his past. Until Alessia had come back into his life, and at the moment all he wanted was for her to be gone, and for his life to go back to the way it had been.

He cupped her chin, tilted her face up so that her eyes met his. "I am not holding you here. I am not your father and I am not your jailer."

Dark eyes met his, the steel in them shocking. "No, you aren't. But you are the father of my baby. Our baby. I'm not going to walk away, Matteo. If you want an out, you'll have to take it yourself. Don't think that I will. I'm strong enough to face this. To try to make this work."

"It would be better if you would."

"Do you really think that?"

"You think I will be a hands-on father? That I will somehow...be an influence in our child's life?" The very thought made him sick. What could he offer a child but a legacy of violence and abuse? But he couldn't walk away, either. Couldn't leave Alessia on her own. But he feared his touch would only poison a child. His baby would be born innocent, unspoiled by the world, and Matteo was supposed to hold him? With his hands? Hands that were stained with blood.

"You think you won't be?"

"How can you give what you never had?"

"I hardly remember my mother, Matteo, but I did a good job with my brothers and sisters."

"Perhaps I find that an absence of a good parent is not the same as having bad ones. What lessons shall I teach our child, *cara*? The kind my father taught me? How to find a man who owes you money? How to break his knee-caps with efficiency when he doesn't pay up? I think not."

He had thought she would look shocked by that, but she hardly flinched, her eyes never wavering from his. "Again you underestimate me, Matteo. You forget the family I come from."

"You are so soft," he said, speaking his mind, speaking his heart. "Breakable. Like a flower. You and I are not the same."

She nodded slowly. "It's easy to crush a flower. But if it's the right kind of flower, it comes back, every year, after every winter. No matter how many times you destroy the surface, it keeps on living underneath."

Her words sent a shot of pain straight to his chest, her quiet strength twisting something deep inside of him. "Don't pretend you were forced into this," he said softly. "You were given your choice."

"And you were given yours."

He nodded once and turned away from her, walked out of the room ignoring the pounding in his blood, ignoring the tightness in his chest. Trying to banish the image of his hand closing around a blossom and crushing the petals, leaving it completely destroyed.

Alessia looked around the lavish, now empty, suite that she was staying in until…until she didn't know when. Weeks of not being able to get ahold of Matteo, not knowing what she would do if she didn't, and now he was suddenly in her life like a hurricane, uprooting everything, taking control of everything.

She really shouldn't be too surprised about it. That was one thing she did know about Matteo Corretti, beyond that stupid ream of noninformation he'd given her. He was controlled. Totally. Completely.

Twice she'd seen him lose that control. Once, on a sunny day in Sicily while he was staying at his grandparents' rural estate. The day that had cemented him in her mind as her potential salvation.

And their night in New York. There had been no control then, not for either of them.

She pictured him as he'd been then. The way he'd

looked at her in the low light of the bar. She closed her eyes and she was back there. The memory still so strong, so painfully sweet.

"What brings you to New York, Alessia?"

"Bachelorette party." It was easy enough to leave out that it was for her. If he didn't know about Alessandro, then she wouldn't tell him.

"Did you order any strippers?"

Her cheeks heated. "No, gosh, why? Are you offering to fill the position?"

"How much have you had to drink?" he asked, a smile on his face. It was so rare for her to see him smile. She couldn't remember if she ever had.

"Not enough."

"I could fix that, but I think I'd like a dance and if you're too drunk you won't be able to keep up."

"Why are you talking to me?" she asked. She'd known there was a chance he could be here. He owned the hotel, after all. Part of her had hoped she'd catch a glimpse of him. A little bit of torture, but torture that would be well worth it.

"What do you mean?"

"You haven't spoken to me since—" something flashed in his eyes, a strange unease, and she redirected her words "—in a long time."

"Too long," he said, his voice rough.

Her heart fluttered, a surge of hope moving through her. She tried to crush it, tried to stop the jittery feelings moving through her now.

"So, do you have a dance for me?" he asked. "For an old friend?"

"Yes." She couldn't deny him, couldn't deny herself.

She left her friends in the corner of the bar, at their table with all of their fruity drinks, and let Matteo lead her away from them, lead her to the darkened dance floor. A jazz quartet was playing, the music slow and sensual.

He wrapped his arms around her waist and pulled her against his body. Heat shot through her, heat and desire and lust.

His eyes locked with hers as they swayed in time to the music, and she was powerless to resist the desire to lean in and press her lips to his. His tongue touched the tip of hers, a shot of need so sharp, so strong, assaulting her she thought it would buckle her knees then and there.

She parted her lips for him, wrapping her arms around his neck, tangling her fingers in his hair. Years of fantasies added fuel to the moment.

Matteo Corretti was her ultimate fantasy. The man whose name she called out in her sleep. The man she wanted, more than anything. And this was her last chance.

Panic drove her, made her desperate. She deepened the kiss, her movements clumsy. She didn't know how to make out. She'd never really done it before. Another thing that added fuel to the fire.

She'd never lived. She'd spent all of her life at the Battaglia *castello*, taking care of her siblings, making sure her family didn't crumble. Her life existed for the comfort of others, and she needed a moment, a night, to have something different.

To have something for her.

Matteo pulled away from her, his chest rising and falling heavily with each indrawn breath. "We cannot do that here."

She shook her head. "Apparently not." The fire between them was burning too hot, too fast, threatening to rage out of control.

"I have a suite." A smile curved his lips. "I own the hotel."

She laughed, nervous, breathless. She flexed her fingers, where her engagement ring should be. The engagement ring she hadn't put on tonight as she'd gotten ready for the party.

"Please. Just one night," she said.

"Only one, *cara mia*?"

"That's all I have to give."

"I might be able to change your mind," he said, his voice rough. He leaned in and kissed her neck, his teeth scraping her delicate skin, his tongue soothing away the sting.

Yes. She wanted to shout it. *Yes, forever. Matteo,* ti amo.

Instead, she kissed him again, long and deep, pouring everything out, every emotion, every longing that had gone unanswered for so long. Every dream she knew would never be fulfilled. Because Matteo might be hers tonight, but in just a month, she would belong to another man forever.

"Take me to your room."

Alessia shook her head, brought herself back to the present. Everything had been so perfect that night. It was the morning that had broken her heart. The cold light of day spilling over her, illuminating the truth, not allowing her to hide behind fantasy any longer.

She could remember just how he'd looked, the sheets tangled around his masculine body, bright white against his dark skin. Leaving him had broken her.

She'd wanted so badly to kiss him again, but she hadn't wanted to chance waking him.

Somehow that night she'd let her fantasies become real, had let them carry her away from reality, not just in her imagination but for real. And she couldn't regret it, not then, not now.

At least, she hadn't until recently. The way Matteo looked at her now...she hated it. Hated that he saw her as a leash.

But it was too late to turn back now. The dutiful daughter had had her rebellion, and it had destroyed everything in its path.

"You don't go halfway, do you, Alessia?" she asked the empty room.

Unsurprisingly, she got no answer.

CHAPTER FIVE

"You cannot simply take what is mine without paying for it, Corretti."

Matteo looked at Antonioni Battaglia and fought a wave of rage. The man had no idea who he was dealing with. Matteo was a Corretti, the capability to commit hideous acts was a part of his DNA. More than that, Matteo had actually done it before. Had embraced the violence. Both with cold precision, and in the heat of rage.

The temptation to do it again was strong. Instead, he leaned forward and adjusted a glass figurine that his grandmother had had commissioned for him. A perfect model of his first hotel. Not one of the Corretti Hotels, the first hotel he'd bought with his own personal fortune.

"And what exactly is that?" Matteo asked, leaning back in his office chair.

"My daughter. You defiled her. She's much less valuable to me now, which means you'd better damn well marry her and make good on the deal I cut with your grandfather, or the Correttis won't be doing any trading out of Sicily."

"My mistake, I thought Alessia's body belonged to her, not you."

"I'm an old-fashioned man."

"Be that as it may, the law prevents you from owning anyone, which means Alessia does not belong to you." He gritted his teeth, thought of Alessia's siblings, of all she'd given up to ensure they would be cared for. "However, at my fiancée's request, I have decided to honor the agreement." He paused for a moment. "What are your other children doing at the moment?"

"I've arranged for the boys to get a job in the family business."

Matteo gritted his teeth. "Is that what they want?"

"You have to take opportunity where it exists."

"And if I created a different opportunity?" He turned the figurine again, keeping his hands busy, keeping himself from violence.

"Why should I do any more business with a Corretti than necessary?"

"Because I hold your potential fortune in the palm of my hands. Not only that, I'll be the father of your first grandchild. Mainly, though, because you'll take what I give you, and no more. So it's by my good grace that you will have anything."

Antonioni's cheeks turned red. It was clear the old man didn't like being told what to do. "Corretti, I don't have to give your family rights to—"

"And I don't have to give you a damn thing. I know you're making deals with Angelo. And you know how I feel about Angelo, which puts you in my bad book right off. I may, however, be willing to overlook it all if you do as I ask. So I suggest you take steps to make me happy. Send your children to college. I'm paying for it."

"That's hardly necessary."

He thought of Alessia, of all she'd sacrificed for them. "Listen to me now, Battaglia, and remember what I say. Memorize it. Make a nice little plaque and hang it above your fireplace if need be: If I say it is necessary, then it is. So long as you do what I say, you'll be kept well in the lifestyle you would like to become accustomed to."

The other man nodded. "It's your dime, Corretti."

"Yes, and your life is now on my dime. Get used to that concept."

Had Alessia's father not said what he had, had he not acted as though her virginity, her body, was his bargaining tool, Matteo might not have taken such joy in letting the other man know his neck was, in effect, under his heel.

But he had. So Matteo did.

"I paid for one wedding," Battaglia said. "I'm not paying for another."

"I think I can handle that, too." Matteo picked up the tiny glass hotel, turning it in front of the light. "You're dismissed."

Battaglia liked that last order least of all, but he complied, leaving Matteo's office without another word.

Matteo tightened his hold on the small, breakable representation of his empire, curling his fingers around it, not stopping until it cracked, driving a shard deep into his palm.

He looked down, watched the blood drip down his wrist. Then he set the figurine back on his desk, examined the broken pieces. Marveled at how easy it was to destroy it with his anger.

He pulled the silk handkerchief out of the pocket of his jacket and wrapped the white fabric around his hand, pressing it hard, until a spot of crimson stained the fabric.

It was so easy to let emotion ruin things. So frighteningly easy.

He gritted his teeth, pushed the wall up around himself again. Control. He would have it, in all things. Alessia Battaglia was not allowed to steal it from him. Not anymore.

Never again.

"I've secured the marriage license, and we will have the wedding at my palazzo." His inheritance after the death of his father. A piece of his childhood he wasn't certain he wanted. But one he possessed nonetheless.

"Not at your family home?"

"I have no use for that place," he said, his tone hard. "Anyway, it has all been arranged."

Alessia stood up from the plush bed, crossing her arms beneath her breasts. "Really? And what shall I wear? How shall I fix my hair? Have you written my vows for me?"

"I don't care. Who gives a damn? And didn't someone already take care of writing vows for weddings hundreds of years ago?"

She blinked, trying to process his rapid-fire response. "I… Don't you have… I mean, don't I need to conform to some sort of image you're projecting or…something?"

"This will be a small affair. We may provide the press with a picture for proof. Or perhaps I'll just send them a photocopy of the marriage license. Anyway, you can wear what you like. I've never seen you not looking beautiful."

The compliment, careless, offhanded, sent a strange sensation through her. "Oh. Well. Thank you."

"It's the truth."

"Well, thank you again."

She wasn't sure what to do, both with him being nice and with him giving her a choice on what to wear to the wedding. Such a simple thing, but it was more than her father had given her when it came to Alessandro.

"As long as it doesn't have lace," she said.

"What?"

"The wedding dress."

"The dress for your last wedding was covered in it."

"Exactly. Hellish, awful contraption. And I didn't choose it. I didn't choose any of that."

"What would you have chosen?"

She shook her head and looked down. "Does it matter?"

"Why not? You can't walk down the aisle naked and

we have to get married somewhere, so you might as well make the choice."

"I would wear something simple. Beautiful. And I would be barefoot. And it would be outside."

He lifted his hand and brushed it over his short hair. "Of course. Then we'll have it outside at the palazzo and you may forego shoes." He lowered his hand and she saw a slash of red on his palm.

She frowned and stepped forward. "What did you do?"

"What?" He turned his hand over. "Nothing. Just a cut."

"You look like you got in a fight."

His whole body tensed. "I don't get in fights."

"No, I know. I wasn't being serious." Tension held between them as they both had the same memory. She knew that was what was happening. Knew that he was thinking of the day she'd been attacked.

But she wanted to know what he remembered, how he remembered it, because it was obvious it was something he preferred to ignore. Not that she loved thinking about it except…except as horrible as it had been to have those men touching her, pawing at her, as awful as those memories were, the moment when they'd been wrenched from her, when she'd seen Matteo…the rush of relief, the feeling of absolute peace and certainty that everything would be okay, had been so real, so acute, she could still feel it.

She'd clung to him after. Clung to him and cried. And he'd stroked her cheek with his hand, wiping away her tears. Later she'd realized he'd left a streak of blood on her face, from the blood on his hands. Blood he'd shed, spilled, for her.

He'd been her hero that day, and every day since. She'd spent her whole life saving everyone else, being the stopgap for her siblings, taking her father's wrath if they'd been too noisy. Always the one to receive a slap across the face, rather than allow him near the younger children.

Matteo was the only person who'd ever stood up for her. The only one who'd ever saved her. And so, when life got hard, when it got painful, or scary, she would imagine that he would come again. That he would pull her into impossibly strong arms and fight her demons for her.

He never did. Never again. After that day, he even stopped watching her. But having the hope of it, the fantasy, was part of what had pulled her through the bleakness of her life. Imagination had always been her escape, and he'd added a richer texture to it, given a face to her dreams for the future.

He'd asked if she always spoke her mind, and she'd told him the truth, she didn't. She kept her head down and tried to get through her life, tried to simply do the best she could. But in her mind…her imagination was her escape, and always had been. When she ran barefoot through the garden, she was somewhere else entirely.

When she went to bed at night, she read until sleep found her, so that she could have new thoughts in her head, rather than simply memories of the day.

So that she could have better dreams.

It was probably a good thing Matteo didn't know the place he occupied in her dreams. It would give him too much power. More than he already had.

"I'm not like my father," he said. "I will never strike my wife."

She looked at him and she realized that never, for one moment, had she believed he would. Her father had kept her mother "in line" with the back of his hand, and he'd done the same with her. But even having grown up with that as a normal occurrence, she'd never once imagined Matteo would do it.

"I know," she said.

"You know?"

"Yes."

"And how is it you know?"

"Because you aren't that kind of person, Matteo."

"Such confidence in me. Especially when you're one of the very few people who has actually seen what I'm capable of."

She had. She'd seen his brute strength applied to those who had dared try to harm her. It had been the most welcome sight in all of her life. "You protected me."

"I went too far."

"They would have gone further," she said.

He took a step away from her, the darkness in his eyes suddenly so deep, so pronounced, it threatened to pull her in. "I have work to do. I'll be at my downtown office. I've arranged to have a credit card issued to you." He reached into his pocket and pulled out a black card, extending his hand to her.

She took it, not ready to fight with him about it.

"If you need anything, whatever you need, it's yours." He turned away and walked out of the room, closing the door behind him.

She'd done the wrong thing again. With Matteo it seemed she could do nothing right. And she so desperately wanted to do right by him.

But it seemed impossible.

She growled, the sound releasing some of her tension. But not enough. "Matteo, why are you always so far out of my reach?"

This was Alessia's second wedding day. Weird, because she'd never technically had a boyfriend. One hot night of sex didn't really make Matteo her boyfriend. *Boyfriend* sounded too tame for a man like Matteo, anyway. Alessia finished zipping up the back of her gown. It was light, with flutter sleeves and a chiffon skirt that swirled around her ankles. It was lavender instead of white. She was a pregnant bride, after all.

There weren't many people in attendance, but she liked that better. Her father, her brothers and sisters, Matteo's grandmother, Teresa, and his mother, Simona.

She took the bouquet of lilacs she'd picked from the garden out of their vase and looked in the mirror. Nothing like what the makeup artist had managed on The Other Wedding Day, but today she at least looked like her.

She opened the guest bedroom door and tried to get a handle on her heart rate.

She was marrying Matteo Corretti today. In a sun-drenched garden. She was having his baby. She repeated that, over and over, trying to make it feel real, trying to hold on to the surge of good feelings it gave her. Because no matter how terrifying it was sometimes, it was also wonderful. A chance at something new. A chance to have a child, give that child the life that had been denied her. The life that had been denied Matteo.

The stone floor was cool beneath her bare feet, the palazzo empty, everyone outside waiting. She'd opted to forego shoes since that was how he said he knew her.

Barefoot in the garden. So, she would meet him as he remembered her. Barefoot in the garden, with her hair down. Maybe then they could start over. They were getting married today, after all, and in her mind that meant they would have to start trying to work things out. They would at least have to be civil.

She put her hands on the rail of the curved, marble staircase, still repeating her mantra. She walked through the grand foyer, decorated in traditional, ornate furniture that didn't remind her one bit of Matteo, and she opened the door, stepping out into the sun.

The music was already playing. A string quartet. She'd

forgotten to say what she wanted for music but this was perfect, simple.

And in spite of what Matteo had said, there was a photographer.

But those details faded into the background when she saw Matteo, standing near the priest, his body rigid, his physique displayed to perfection by a custom-made gray suit.

There was no aisle. No loud click of marble beneath her heels, just grass beneath her feet. And the guests were standing, no chairs. Her father looked like he was ready to grab her if she decided to run. Eva, Giana, Pietro and Marco looked worried, and she didn't blame them. She had been their stability for most of their lives, their surrogate mother. And she hadn't told them she was marrying Alessandro for convenience, which meant her disappearance, subsequent reappearance with a different groom and a publicly announced pregnancy must seem a few steps beyond bizarre to them.

She gave them her best, most confident smile. This was her role. To show them it was all okay, to hold everything together.

But her eyes were drawn back to Matteo. He made her throat dry, made her heart pound.

But when she reached him, he didn't take her hand. He hardly looked at her. Instead, he looked at the priest. The words to the ceremony were traditional, words she knew by heart from attending hundreds of society weddings in her life.

There was nothing personal about them, nothing unique. And Matteo never once met her eyes.

She was afraid she was alone in her resolve to make things work. To make things happy. She swallowed hard. It was always her job to make it okay. To smooth it over. Why wasn't it working?

"You may kiss the bride."

They were the words she'd been anticipating and dreading. She let her eyes drift shut and she waited. She could feel his heat draw near to her, and then, the brush of his lips on hers, so soft, so brief, she thought she might have imagined it.

And then nothing more.

Her breath caught, her heart stopped. She opened her eyes, and Matteo was already turning to face their small audience. Then he drew her near to him, his arm tight around her waist. But there was no intimacy in the gesture. No warmth.

"Thank you for bearing witness," Matteo said, both to her father and his grandmother.

"You've done a good thing for the family, Matteo," his grandmother said, putting a hand over his. And Alessia wondered just how much trouble Matteo had been in with his family for the wedding fiasco.

She knew the media had made assumptions they'd run off together. Too bad nothing could be further from the truth.

Still, her father, his family, must think that was the truth. Because now they were back in Sicily, she was pregnant and they were married.

"Perhaps we should go inside for a drink?" her father suggested.

"A good plan, Battaglia, but we don't talk business at weddings."

Simona begged off, giving Matteo a double kiss on the cheeks and saying she had a party to get to in the city. Matteo didn't seem the least bit fazed by his mother's abandonment. He simply followed her father into the house.

She watched him walk inside, her heart feeling heavy.

Teresa offered her a smile. "I'll see that Matteo's staff finds some refreshments to serve for us. I'll only be a moment." The older woman turned and went into the house, too, leaving Alessia with her siblings.

It was Eva, fourteen and emotional, who flung herself into Alessia's arms. "Where did you go?"

"New York," Alessia said, stroking her sister's hair.

"Why?"

"I had to get away...I couldn't marry Alessandro."

"Then why did you agree to the engagement?" This from Marco, the second oldest at nineteen.

"It's complicated, Marco, as things often are with Father. You know that."

"But you wanted to marry Corretti? This Corretti, I mean," asked sixteen-year-old Pietro.

She nodded, her throat tight. "Of course." She didn't want them to be upset. Didn't want them to worry. She maybe should have thought of that before running off to New York, but she really hadn't been able to consider anyone else. For the first time, she'd been burned out on it and she'd had to take care of herself.

"They're having a baby," Giana said drily. "I assume that means she liked him at least a little bit." Then she turned back to Alessia. "I'm excited about being an aunt."

"I'm glad," she said, tugging on her sister's braid.

They spent the rest of the afternoon out in the garden, having antipasti, wine for the older children and Teresa, and lemonade for her and younger kids. Her siblings told her stories of their most recent adventures, which ended up with everyone laughing. And for the first time in months, Alessia felt at ease. This was her family, her happiness. The reason she'd agreed to marry Alessandro. And one of the driving reasons behind her decision to marry Matteo.

Although she couldn't deny her own desire where he was concerned. Still, *happy* wasn't exactly the word that she would use to describe herself at the moment. Anxiety-ridden? Check. Sick to her stomach? That a little bit, too.

The sun was starting to sink behind the hills, gray twilight settling on the garden, the solar lights that were strung across the expanse of the grass illuminating the growing darkness.

Their father appeared on the balcony, his arms folded across his chest, his eyes settled on her siblings.

"I guess we have to go," Marco said.

"I know. Come back and stay with us anytime," she said, not even thinking to ask Matteo if it was okay. As soon as she had the thought, she banished it. If she was going to be married to the man, then she wasn't going to ask his permission to breathe in their shared home. It wasn't only his now and he would have to get used to it.

Her father was the unquestionable head of their household, but she was the heart of it. She'd kept it running, made sure the kids got their favorite meals cooked, remembered birthdays and helped with homework. Her role in their lives didn't end with her marriage, and she wasn't equipped to take on a passive role in a household, anyway.

So, on that, Matteo would just have to learn to deal.

She stopped and kissed her brothers and sisters on the head before watching them go up to where their father stood. All of them but Marco. She held him a bit longer in her embrace. "Take care of everyone," she said, a tear escaping and sliding down her cheek.

"Just like you always did," he said softly.

"And I'm still here."

"I know."

He squeezed her hand before walking up to join the rest of the family.

"And I should leave you, as well," Teresa said, standing. "It was lovely to see you again, my dear."

Teresa hadn't batted an eye at the sudden change of groom, had never seemed at all ruffled by the events.

"You care for him," she said, as if she could read Alessia's internal musings.

Alessia nodded. "I do."

"That's what these men need, Alessia. A strong woman to love them. They may fight it, but it is what they need." Teresa spoke with pain in her eyes, a pain that Alessia felt echo inside of her.

Alessia couldn't speak past the lump in her throat. She tried to avoid the *L* word. The one that was stronger than *like*. There was only so much a woman could deal with at once. So instead, she just nodded and watched Teresa walk back up toward the house.

Alessia stayed in the garden and waited. The darkness thickened, the lights burning brighter. And Matteo didn't come.

She moved into the house, walked up the stairs. The palazzo was completely quiet, the lights off. She wrapped her arms around herself, and made her way back to the bedroom Matteo had put her in to get ready.

She went in and sat on the edge of the bed and waited for her husband to come and claim his wedding night.

CHAPTER SIX

MATTEO DIDN'T GET DRUNK as a rule. Unfortunately, he had a tendency to break rules when Alessia Battaglia—or was she Alessia Corretti now?—was involved.

Damn that woman.

Even after his father's death he hadn't gotten drunk. He'd wanted to. Had wanted to incinerate the memories, destroy them as the fire had destroyed the warehouses, destroyed the man who had held so much sway over his life.

But he hadn't. Because he hadn't deserved that kind of comfort. That kind of oblivion. He'd forced himself to face it.

This...this he couldn't face.

He took another shot of whiskey and let it burn all the way down. It didn't burn as much at this point in the evening, which was something of a disappointment. He looked down at the shot glass and frowned. Then he picked it up and threw it against the wall, watching the glass burst.

Now that was satisfying.

He chuckled and lifted the bottle to his lips. *Dio*, in his current state he almost felt happy. Why the hell didn't he drink more?

"Matteo?"

He turned and saw Alessia standing in the doorway. Alessia. He wanted her. More than his next breath. He wanted those long legs wrapped around his waist, wanted to hear her husky voice whispering dirty things in his ear.

He didn't think she'd ever done that, whispered dirty things in his ear, but he could imagine it, and he wanted it. *Dio*, did he want it.

"Come here, wife," he said, pushing away from the bar, his movements unsteady.

"Are you drunk?"

"I should be. If I'm not…if I'm not there's something very wrong with this whiskey."

Her dark eyes were filled with some kind of emotion. Something strong and deep. He couldn't decipher it. He didn't want to.

"Why are you drunk?"

"Because I've been drinking. Alcohol. A lot of it."

"But why?"

"I don't know, could be because today I acquired a wife and I can't say I ever particularly wanted one."

"Thank you. I'm so glad to hear that, after the cere-mony."

"You would have changed your mind? You can't. It's all over the papers, in the news all over the world. You're carrying a Corretti. You, a Battaglia. It's news, *cara*. Not since Romeo and Juliet has there been such a scandal."

"I'm not going to stab myself for you just because you've poisoned your damn self, so you can stop making those parallels anytime."

"Come to me, Alessia."

She took a step toward him, her movements unsteady, her lips turned down into a sulky frown. He wanted to kiss the expression off her face.

"You left your hair down," he said, reaching out and tak-ing a dark lock between his thumb and forefinger, rubbing the glossy strands. "You're so beautiful. An angel. That was the first thing I thought when I saw you."

She blinked rapidly. "When?"

"When we were children. I had always been told you Battaglias were monsters. Demons. And I couldn't resist the chance to peek. And there you were, running around your father's garden. You were maybe eleven. You were dirty and your hair was tangled, but I thought you looked like heaven. You were smiling. You always smile." He frowned, looking at her face again. "You don't smile as much now."

"I haven't had a lot of reasons to smile."

"Have you ever?"

"No. But I've made them. Because someone had to smile. Someone had to teach the children how to smile."

"And it had to be you?"

"There was no one else."

"So you carry the weight of the world, little one?"

"You should know something about that, Matteo."

He chuckled. "Perhaps a little something." He didn't feel so much like he was carrying it now.

He took her arm and tugged her forward, her dark eyes wide. "I want you," he said.

Not waiting for a response, he leaned in and kissed her. Hard. She remained immobile beneath his mouth, her lips stiff, her entire body stiff. He pulled her more firmly against him, let her feel the evidence of his arousal, let her feel all of the frustration and need that had been building inside of him for the past three months.

"Did he kiss you like this?" he asked, pressing a heated kiss to her neck, her collarbone.

She shook her head. "N-no."

"Good. I would have had to kill him."

"Stop saying things like that."

"Why?" he asked. "You and I both know that I could, Alessia. On your behalf, I could. I might not even be able to stop myself." He kissed her again, his heart pounding hard, blood pouring hot and fast through his veins.

"Matteo, stop," she said, pulling away from him.

"Why? Are you afraid of me, too, Alessia?"

She shook her head. "No, but you aren't yourself. I don't like it."

"Maybe I am myself, and in that case, you're wise not to like it."

He released his hold on her. And he realized how tight his grip had been. Regret, the kind he usually kept dammed up inside of himself, released, flooding through him. "Did I hurt you?"

She shook her head. "No."

"Don't lie."

"I wouldn't."

Suddenly, he was hit with a shot of self-realization so strong it nearly buckled his knees. He had done it again. He had let his defenses down with Alessia. Let them? He didn't allow anything, with her it was just total destruction, a sudden, real demolition that he didn't seem to be able to control at all.

"Get out," he said.

"Matteo..."

"Out!" he roared, images flashing before his eyes. Images of violence. Of bones crushing beneath his fists, of not being able to stop. Not being able to stop until he was certain they could never hurt her again.

And it melded with images of his father. His father beating men until they were unconscious. Until they didn't get back up again.

"What did they do?"

"They didn't pay."

"Is that all?"

"Is that all? Matteo, you can't let anyone disrespect you, ever. Otherwise, it gets around. You have to make them an

example. Whatever you have to do to protect your power, you do it. And if people have to die to secure it, so be it. Casualties of war, figlio mio.*"

No. He wasn't like that.

But you were, Matteo. You are.

Then in his mind, it wasn't his father doing the beating. It was him.

"Out!"

Alessia's dark eyes widened and she backed out of the room, a tear tracking down her cheek.

He sank down into a chair, his fingers curled tightly around a bottle of whiskey as the edges of his vision turned fuzzy, darkened.

Che cavolo, what was she doing to him?

Alessia slammed the bedroom door behind her and tore at the back of her wedding dress, such as it was, sobbing as she released the zipper and let it fall to the floor. She'd wanted Matteo to be the one to take it off her. She hadn't realized how much until now.

Instead, her groom was off getting drunk rather than dealing with her.

"It's more than that," she said out loud. And she knew that it was. He was getting drunk instead of dealing with a whole lot of things.

Well, it was unfair because she couldn't get drunk. She was pregnant with the man's baby, and while he numbed the pain of it all, she just had to stand around and endure it.

There was nothing new to that. She had to smile. Had to keep it all moving.

She sat down on the edge of the bed, then scooted into the middle of it, lying down, curling her knees into her chest. Tonight, there was no fantasy to save her, no way to avoid reality.

Matteo had long been her rescue from the harsh reality

and pain of life. And now he was her harsh reality. And he wasn't who she'd believed he was. She'd simplified him, painted him as a savior.

She'd never realized how much he needed to be saved. The question was, was she up to the challenge? No, the real question was, did she have a choice?

There wasn't a word foul enough to help release the pain that was currently pounding through Matteo's head. So he said them all.

Matteo sat upright in the chair. He looked down at the floor, there was a mostly empty whiskey bottle lying on its side by the armchair. And there was a dark star-shaped whiskey stain on the wall, glass shards gathered beneath.

He remembered…not very much. The wedding. He was married now. He looked down at the ring on his left hand. Yes, he was married now.

He closed his eyes again, trying to lessen the pain in his head, and had a flash of lilac memory. A cloud of purple, long dark hair. He'd held her arm and pulled her against him, his lips hard on hers.

Dio, what had he done? Where had it stopped? He searched his brain desperately for an answer, tried to figure out what he'd done. What she'd done.

He stood quickly, ignoring the dizziness, the ferocious hammering in his temples. He swore again as he took his first step, he legs unsteady beneath him.

What was his problem? Where was his control? He knew better than to drink like that, knew better than to allow any lowered inhibitions.

The first time he'd gotten that drunk had been the night following Alessia's rescue. He hadn't been able to get clean. Hadn't been able to get the images out of his head. Images of what he was capable of.

The stark truth was, it hadn't been the attack that had

driven him to drink. It had been what his father had said afterward.

"You are my son."

When Benito Corretti had seen his son, blood-streaked, after the confrontation with Alessia's attackers, he'd assumed that it meant Matteo was finally following in his footsteps. Had taken it as confirmation.

But Matteo hadn't. It had been six years after that night when Benito had said it to him again. And that night, Matteo had embraced the words, and proven the old man right.

He pushed the memories away, his heart pounding too hard to go there.

He knew full well that he was capable of unthinkable things, even without the loss of control. But when control was gone…when it was gone, he truly became a monster. And last night, he'd lost control around Alessia.

He had to find her.

He walked down the hall, his heart pounding a sick tempo in his skull, his entire body filled with lead.

He went down the stairs, the natural light filtering through the windows delivering a just punishment for his hideous actions.

Coffee. He would find coffee first, and then Alessia.

He stopped when he got to the dining room. It turned out he had found both at the same time.

"Good morning," Alessia said, her hands folded in front of her, her voice soft and still too loud.

"Morning," he said, refusing to call it good.

"I assume you need coffee?" she asked, indicating a French press, ready for brewing, and a cup sitting next to it.

"Yes."

"You know how that works, right?" she asked.

"Yes."

"Good."

She didn't make a move to do it for him, she simply sat in her seat, drinking a cup of tea.

He went to his spot at the expansive table, a few seats away from hers, and sat, pushing the plunger down slowly on the French press.

He poured himself a cup, left it black. He took a drink and waited a moment, letting the strong brew do its magic.

"Alessia," he said, his voice rusty, the whiskey burn seeming to linger, "last night...did I hurt you?"

"In what way?" she asked, leaning back in her chair, her dark eyes unflinching.

"Physically."

"No."

The wave of relief that washed over him was profound, strong. "I'm pleased to hear it."

"Emotionally, on the other hand, I'm not sure I faired so well."

"Why is that?"

"Well, let's see, my husband got drunk on our wedding night instead of coming to bed with me. What do you think?"

"I'm sorry if I wounded your pride," he said, "that wasn't my intention." What he'd been after was oblivion, which he should have known wasn't a safe pursuit.

"Wouldn't your pride have been wounded if I'd done the same?"

"I would have ripped the bottle out of your hand. You're pregnant."

There hadn't been a lot of time for him to really pause and think through the implications of that. It had all been about securing the marriage. Staying a step ahead of the press at all times. Making sure Alessia was legally bound to him.

"Hence the herbal tea," she said, raising her cup to him. "And the pregnancy wasn't really my point."

"Alessia…this can't be a normal marriage."

"Why not?" she asked, sitting up straighter.

"Because it simply can't be. I'm a busy man, I travel a lot. I was never going to marry…I never would have married."

"I don't see why we can't have a normal marriage anyway. A lot of men and women travel for business, it doesn't mean they don't get married."

"I don't love you."

Alessia felt like he'd slapped her. His words were so bald, so true and unflinching. And they cut a swath of devastation through her. "I didn't ask you to," she said, because it was the only truth she could bring herself to speak.

"Perhaps not, but a wife expects it from her husband."

"I doubt my father loved my mother, and if he did, it wasn't the kind of love I would like to submit to. What about yours?"

"*Obsession,* perhaps, was a better word. My father loved Lia's mother, I'm sure of that. I'm not certain he loved mine. At least, not enough to stay away from other women. And my mother was—is, for that matter—very good at escaping unpleasant truths by way of drugs and alcohol." His headache mocked him, a reminder that he'd used alcohol for the very same reason last night.

"Perhaps it was their marriages that weren't normal. Perhaps—"

"Alessia, don't. I think you saw last night that I'm not exactly a brilliant candidate for husband or father of the year."

"So try to be. Don't just tell me you can't, Matteo, or that you don't want to. Be better. That's what I'm trying to do. I'm trying to be stronger, to do the right thing."

"Yes, because that's what you do," he said, his tone dry. "You make things better, because it makes you feel better, and as long as you feel good you assume all is right with your world. You trust your moral compass."

"Well, yes, I suppose that's true."

"I don't trust mine. I want things I shouldn't want. I have already taken what I didn't have the right to take."

"If you mean my virginity, I will throw this herbal tea in your face," she said, pregnancy hormones coming to the rescue, bringing an intense surge of anger.

"I'm not so crass, but yes. Your body, you, you aren't for me."

"For Alessandro? That's who I was for?"

"That isn't what I meant."

"The hell it's not, Matteo!" she shouted, not caring if she hurt his head. Him and his head could go to hell. "You're just like him. You think I can't make my own decisions? That I don't know my own mind? My body belongs to me, not to you, not to my father, not to Alessandro. I didn't give myself to you, I took you. I made you tremble beneath my hands, and I could do it again. Don't treat me like some fragile thing. Don't treat me like you have to protect me from myself."

He stayed calm, maddeningly so, his focus on his cup of coffee. "It's not you I'm protecting you from."

"It's you?"

A smile, void of humor, curved his lips. "I don't trust me, Alessia, why should you?"

"Well, let me put you at ease, Matteo. I don't trust anyone. Just because I jumped into bed with you doesn't mean you're the exception. I just think you're hot." She was minimizing it. Minimizing what she felt. And she hated that. But she was powerless to do anything to stop the words from coming out. She wanted to protect herself, to push him back from her vulnerable places. To keep him from hurting her.

Because the loss of Matteo in her fantasies…it was almost too much to bear. As he became her reality, she was losing her escape, and she was angry at him for taking it. For not being the ideal she had made him out to be.

"I'm flattered," he said, taking another drink of his coffee.

"How do you see this marriage going, then?"

"I don't want to hurt you."

"Assume it's too late. Where do we go from here?"

He leaned forward, his dark eyes shuttered. "When exactly are you due?"

"November 22. It was easy for them to figure out since I knew the exact date I conceived."

"I will make sure you get the best care, whatever you need. And we'll make a room for the baby."

"Well, all things considered, I suppose our child should have a room in his own house."

"I'm trying," he bit out. "I'm not made for this. I don't know how to handle it."

"Well, I do. I know exactly how much work babies are. I know exactly what it's like to raise children. I was thirteen when my mother died. Thirteen when my baby sister and the rest of my siblings became my responsibility. Babies are hard work. But you love them, so much. And at the same time, they take everything from you. I know that, I know it so well. And I'm terrified," she said, the last word breaking. It was a horrible confession, but it was true.

She'd essentially raised four children, one of them from infancy, and as much as she adored them, with every piece of herself, she also knew the cost of it. Knew just how much you poured into children. How much you gave, how much they took.

And she was doing it again. Without ever finding a place for herself in the world. Without having the fantasies she'd craved. True love. A man who would take care of her.

You've had some of the fantasies.

Oh, yes, she had. But one night of passion wasn't the sum total of her life's desires.

"All of this," he said. "And still you want this child?"

"Yes, Matteo. I do. Because babies are a lot of work. But the love you feel for them...it's stronger than anything, than any fear. It doesn't mean I'm not afraid, only that I know in the end the love will win."

"Well, we can be terrified together," he said.

"You're terrified?"

"Babies are tiny. They look very easily broken."

"I'll teach you how to hold one."

Their eyes met, heat arching between them, and this time her pregnancy hormones were making her feel something other than anger.

She looked back down at her breakfast. "How's your head?"

"I feel like someone put a woodpecker in my skull."

"It's no less than you deserve."

"I will treat you better than I did last night. That I promise you. I'm not sure what other promises I can make, but that one...that one I will keep."

She thought of him last night. Broken. Passionate. Needy. She wondered how much of that was the real Matteo. How much he kept hidden beneath a facade.

How much he kept from escaping. And she knew just how he felt in some ways. Knew what it was like to hide everything behind a mask. It was just that her mask was smiling, and his hardly made an expression at all.

"Will you be faithful to me?" she asked, the words catching in her throat.

Matteo looked down into his coffee for a moment, then stood, his cup in his hand. "I have some work to see to this morning, and my head is killing me. We can talk more later."

Alessia's heart squeezed tight, nausea rolling through her. "Later?"

"My head, Alessia."

My heart, you jackass. "Great. Well, perhaps we can have a meeting tonight, or something."

"We're busy tonight."

"Oh. Doing what?"

"Celebrating our marriage, quite publicly, at a charity event."

"What?" She felt far too raw to be in public.

"After what happened with Alessandro, we have to present a united front. Your not-quite wedding to him was very public, as was your announcement of your pregnancy. The entire world is very likely scratching their heads over the spectacle we've created, and now it's time to show a little bit of normal."

"But we don't have a normal marriage—I mean, so I've been told."

"As far as the media is concerned we do."

"Why? Afraid of a little scandal? You're a Corretti."

"What do you want our child to grow up and read? Because thanks to the internet, this stuff doesn't die. It's going to linger, scandal following him wherever he goes. You and I both know what that's like. To have all the other kids whisper about your parents. For our part, we aren't criminals, but we've hardly given our child a clean start."

"So we go out and look pretty and sparkly and together, and what? The press just forgets about what happened?"

"No, but perhaps they will continue on in the vein that they've started in."

"What's that?" She'd, frankly, spent a lot of energy avoiding the stories that the media had written about the wedding.

"That we were forbidden lovers, who risked it all to be together."

It wasn't far from the truth, although Matteo hadn't truly known the risk they'd been taking their night together. But she had. And she'd risked it all for the chance to be with him.

Looking at him now, dealing with all the bruises he'd inflicted on her heart, she knew she would make the same choice now. Because at least it had been her choice. Her mistake. Her very first big one. It was like a rite of passage in a way.

"Well, then, I suppose we had better get ready to put on a show. I'm not sure I have the appropriate costume, though."

"I'm sure I can come up with something."

CHAPTER SEVEN

"SOMETHING" TURNED OUT to be an evening gown from the Corretti fashion line. It was gorgeous, and it was very slinky, with silky gold fabric that molded to her curves and showed the emerging baby bump that she almost hadn't noticed until she'd put on the formfitting garment.

Of course, there was no point in hiding her pregnancy. She'd announced it on television, for heaven's sake. But even so, since she hadn't really dealt with it yet, she felt nervous about sharing it with the public like this.

She put her hand on her stomach, smoothing her palm over the small bump. She was going to be a mother. Such a frightening, amazing thing to realize. She'd been tangled up in finding Matteo, and then in the days since—had it really only been days?—she'd been dealing with having him back in her life. With marrying him. She hadn't had a chance to really think of the baby in concrete terms.

Alessia looked at herself in the mirror one more time, at her stomach, and then back at her face. Her looks had never mattered very much to her. She was comfortable with them, more or less. She was taller than almost every other woman she knew, and a good portion of the men, at an Amazonian six feet, but Matteo was taller.

He managed to make her feel small. Feminine. Beautiful.

That night they were together he'd made her feel especially beautiful. And then last night he'd made her feel especially undesirable. Funny how that worked.

She turned away from the mirror and walked out of the bedroom. Matteo was standing in the hall waiting for her, looking so handsome in his black suit she went a little weak-kneed. He was a man who had a strong effect, that was for sure.

"Don't you clean up nice," she said. "You almost look civilized."

"Appearances can be deceiving," he said.

"The devil wore Armani?"

"Something like that." He held his hand out and she hesitated for a moment before taking it and allowing him to lead her down the curved staircase and into the foyer. He opened the door for her, his actions that of a perfectly solicitous husband.

Matteo's sports car was waiting for them, the keys in the ignition.

Alessia waited until they were on the road before speaking again. "So, what's the charity?"

He shifted gears, his shoulders bunched up, muscles tense. "It's one of mine."

"You have charities?"

"Yes."

"I didn't realize."

"I thought you knew me."

"We're filled with surprises for each other, aren't we? It's a good thing we have a whole lifetime together to look forward to," she said drily.

"Yes," he said, his voice rough, unconvincing.

And she was reminded of their earlier conversation in the dining room. She'd asked him point-blank if he would be faithful, and he'd sidestepped her. She had a feeling he was doing it again.

She gritted her teeth to keep from saying anything

more. To keep from asking him anything, or pressing the issue. She had some pride. She did. She was sure she did, and she was going to do everything she could to hold on to her last little bit of it.

"Well, what is your charity for, then?"

"This is an education fund. For the schools here."

"That's…great," she said. "I didn't get to do any higher education."

"Did you want to?"

"I don't know. I don't think so. I mean…I didn't really have anything I wanted to be when I grew up."

"Nothing?"

"There weren't a lot of options on the table. Though I did always think I would like to be a mother." A wife and a mother. That she would like to have someone who loved her, cherished her like the men in her much-loved books cherished their heroines. It was a small dream, one that should have been somewhat manageable.

Instead, she'd gone off and traded it in for a night of wild sex.

And darn it, she still didn't regret it. Mainly.

"Mission accomplished."

"Why, yes, Matteo, I am, as they say, living the dream."

"There's no need to be—"

"There is every need to be," she said. "Don't act like I should thank you for any of this."

"I wasn't going to," he said, his tone biting.

"You were headed there. This is not my dream." But it was close. So close that it hurt worse in some ways than not getting anywhere near it at all. Because this was proving that her dream didn't exist. That it wasn't possible.

"My apologies, *cara*, for not being your dream." His voice was rough, angry, and she wanted to know where he got off being mad after the way he'd been treating her.

"And my apologies for not being yours. I imagine if I

had a room number stapled to my forehead and a bag of money in my hand I'd come a little closer."

"Now you're being absurd."

"I don't think so."

Matteo maneuvered his car through the narrow city streets, not bothering with nice things like braking before turning, and pulled up to the front of his hotel.

"It's at your hotel," she said.

"Naturally." He threw the car into Park, then got out, rounding to the passenger side and opening the door for her. "Come, my darling wife, we have a public to impress."

He extended his hand to her and she slowly reached her hand out to accept it. Lighting streaked through her, from her fingertips, spreading to every other part of her, the shock and electricity curling her toes in her pumps.

She stood, her eyes level with his thanks to her shoes. "Thank you."

A member of the hotel staff came to where they were and had a brief exchange with Matteo before getting into the car and driving it off to the parking lot. Alessia wandered to the steps of the hotel, taking two of them before pausing to wait for her husband.

Matteo turned back to her, his dark eyes glittering in the streetlamps. He moved to the stairs, and she advanced up one more, just to keep her height advantage. But Matteo wasn't having it. He got onto her stair, meeting her eyes straight on.

"There are rules tonight, Alessia, and you will play by them."

"Will I?" she asked. She wasn't sure why she was goading him. Maybe because it was the only way in all the world she could feel like she had some power. Or maybe it was because if she wasn't trying to goad him, she was longing for him. And the longing was just unacceptable.

A smile curved his lips and she couldn't help but wonder if he needed this, too. This edge of hostility, the bite of anger between them.

Although why Matteo would need anything to hold her at a distance when he'd already made his feelings quite clear was a mystery to her.

"Yes, my darling wife, you will." He put his hand on her chin, drawing close to her, his heat making her shiver deep inside. It brought her right back to that night.

To the aching, heart-rending desperation she'd felt when his lips had finally touched hers. To the moment they'd closed his hotel room door and he'd pressed her against the wall, devouring, taking, giving.

He drew his thumb across her lower lip and she snapped back to the present. "You must stop looking at me like that," he said.

"Like what?"

"Like you're frightened of me." There was an underlying note to his voice that she couldn't guess at, a frayed edge to his control that made his words gritty.

"I'm not."

"You look at me like I'm the very devil sometimes."

"You act like the very devil sometimes."

"True enough. But there are other times…"

"What other times?"

"You didn't used to look at me that way."

"How did I look at you?" she asked, her chest tightening, her stomach pulling in on itself.

"When you were a girl? With curiosity. At the hotel? Like you were hungry."

"You looked at me the same way."

"And how do you think I look at you now?"

"You don't," she whispered. "When you can help it, you don't look at me at all."

He moved his other hand up to cup her cheek, his thumb still stroking her lower lip. "I'm looking at you now."

And there was heat in his eyes. Heat like there had been their night together, the night that had started all of this. The night that had changed the course of her life.

"Because you have to," she said. "For the guests."

"Oh, yes, the guests," he said.

Suddenly, a flash pierced the dim light, interrupting their moment. They both looked in the direction of the photographer, who was still snapping pictures in spite of the fact that the moment was completely broken.

"Shall we go in?" he asked. Any evidence of frayed control was gone now, the rawness, the intensity, covered by a mask. And now her husband was replaced with a smooth, cool stranger.

She'd love to say it wasn't the man she'd married, but this was exactly the man she'd married. This guarded man with more layers of artifice than anyone she'd ever met. She had been so convinced she'd seen the man behind the fiction, that the night in the hotel she'd seen the real Matteo. That in those stolen glances they'd shared when they were young, she'd seen the truth.

That in the moment of unrestrained violence, when he'd put himself in harm's way to keep her from getting hurt, she'd seen the real man.

Now she realized what small moments those were in the entirety of Matteo's life. And for the first time, she wondered if she was simply wrong about him.

A feeling that settled sickly in her stomach, a leaden weight, as they continued up the stairs and into the entrance to the hotel's main ballroom.

There were more photographers inside, capturing photographs of the well-dressed crème de la crème of Sicilian society. And Alessia did her best to keep a smile on her face. This was her strength, being happy no matter what was going on. Keeping a smile glued to her face at whatever event she was at on behalf of her father, making sure she showed her brothers and sisters she was okay even if she'd just taken a slap to the face from their father.

But this wasn't so simple. She was having a harder time finding a place to go to inside of herself. Having a harder time finding that false feeling of hope that she'd become so good at creating for herself to help preserve her sanity.

No one could live in total hopelessness, so she'd spent her life creating hope inside of herself. She'd managed to do it through so many difficult scenarios. Why was it so hard now? So hard with Matteo?

She knew she'd already answered that question. It was too hard to retreat to a much-loved fantasy when that much-loved fantasy was standing beside you, the source of most of your angst.

Though she couldn't blame it all on Matteo. The night of her bachelorette party was the first night she'd stopped trying to find solace in herself, had stopped just trying to be happy no matter what, and had gone for what she wanted, in spite of possible consequences.

She spent the night with Matteo's arm wrapped around her waist, his touch keeping her entire body strung tight, on a slow burn. She also turned down champagne more times than she could count. Was she normally offered alcohol so much at a party? She'd never been conscious of it when she was allowed to drink it. Right now it just seemed a cruelty, since she could use the haze, but couldn't take the chance with her baby's health.

Anyway, for some reason it all smelled sour and spoiled to her now. The pregnancy was making her nose do weird things.

Although Matteo smelled just as good as he ever had. The thought made her draw a little closer to him, breathe in the scent of him, some sort of spicy cologne mingling with the scent of his skin. She was especially tuned into the scent of his skin now, the scent of his sweat.

Dio, even his sweat turned her on. Because it reminded her of his bare skin, slick from exertion, her hands roaming over his back as he thrust hard into her, his dark eyes intent on hers. And there were no walls. Not then.

She blinked and came back to the present. She really had to stop with the sexual fantasies, they did her no good.

A photographer approached them. "Smile for me?" he asked.

Matteo drew her in close to his body, and she put her hand on his chest. She knew her smile looked perfect. She had perfected her picture smile for events such as these, to put on a good front for the Battaglia family. She was an expert.

Matteo should have been, as well, but he looked like he was trying to smile around a rock in his mouth, his expression strained and unnatural.

"A dance for the new bride and groom?" the photographer asked while taking their picture, and she was sure that in that moment her smile faltered a bit.

"Of course," Matteo said, his grin widening. Was she the only one who could see the totally feral light in his eyes, who could see that none of this was real?

The photographer was smiling back, as were some of the guests standing in their immediate area, so they must not be able to tell. Must not be able to see how completely disingenuous the expression of warmth was.

"Come. Dance with me."

And so she followed him out onto the glossy marble dance floor, where other couples were holding each other close, slow dancing to a piece of piano music.

It was different from when they'd danced in New York. The ballroom was bright, crystal chandeliers hanging overhead, casting shimmering light onto caramel-colored walls and floors. The music was as bright as the lighting, nothing darkly sensual or seductive.

And yet when Matteo drew her into his hold, his arms tight, strong around her, they might as well have been the only two people in the room. Back again, shrouded in darkness in the corner of a club, stealing whatever moments together they could have before fate would force them to part forever.

Except fate had had other ideas.

She'd spent a lot of her life believing in fate, believing that the right thing would happen in the end. She questioned that now. Now she just wondered if she'd let her body lead her into an impossible situation all for the sake of assuaging rioting hormones.

"This will make a nice headline, don't you think?" he asked, swirling her around before drawing her back in tight against him.

"I imagine it will. You're a great dancer, by the way. I don't know if I mentioned that…last time."

"You didn't, but your mouth was otherwise occupied."

Her cheeks heated. "Yes, I suppose it was."

"My mother made sure I had dance lessons starting at an early age. All a part of grooming me to take my place at the helm of Benito's empire."

"But you haven't really. Taken the helm of your father's empire, I mean."

"Not as such. We've all taken a piece of it, but in the meantime we've been working to root out the shadier elements of the business. It's one thing my brothers and I do not suffer. We're not criminals."

"A fact I appreciate. And for the record, neither is Alessandro. I would never have agreed to marry him otherwise."

"Is that so?"

"I've had enough shady dealings to last me a lifetime. My father, for all that he puts on the front of being an honorable citizen, is not. At least your father and your grandfather had the decency to be somewhat open about the fact that they weren't playing by the rules."

"Gentleman thugs," he said, his voice hard. "But I'll let you in on a little secret—no matter how good you are at dancing, no matter how nicely tailored your suit is, it doesn't change the fact that when you hit a man in the legs with a metal cane, his knees shatter. And he doesn't care what you're wearing. Neither do the widows of the men you kill."

Alessia was stunned by his words, not by the content of them, not as shocked as she wished she were. People often assumed that she was some naive, cosseted flower. Her smile had that effect. They assumed she must not know how organized crime worked. But she did. She knew the reality of it. She knew her father was bound up so tightly in all of it he could hardly escape it even if he wanted to.

He was addicted to the power, and being friendly with the mob bosses was what kept him in power. He couldn't walk away easily. Not with his power, possibly not even with his life.

And yet, the Correttis had disentangled themselves from it. The Corretti men and women had walked away from it.

No, it wasn't the content of his words that had surprised her. It was the fact that he'd said them at all. Because Matteo played his cards close to his chest. Because Matteo preferred not to address the subject of his family, of that part of his past.

"You aren't like that, though."

"No?" he asked. "I'm in a suit."

"And you wouldn't do that to someone."

"Darling Alessia, you are an eternal optimist," he said, and there was something in his words she didn't like. A hard edge that made her stomach tighten. "I don't know how you manage it."

"Survival. I have to protect myself."

"I thought that was where cynics came from?"

"Perhaps a good number of them. But no matter how I feel about a situation, I've never had any control over the outcome. My mother died in childbirth, and no amount of feeling good or bad about it would have changed that. My father is a criminal, no matter the public mask he wears, who has no qualms about slapping my face to keep me in line." They swirled in a fast circle, Matteo's hold tightening on her, something dangerous flickering in his eyes. "No matter how I feel about the situation, that is the situation. If I didn't choose to be happy no matter what, I'm not sure I would have ever stopped crying, and I didn't want to live like that, either."

"And why didn't you leave?" he asked.

"Without Marco, Giana, Eva and Pietro? Never. I couldn't do it."

"With them, then."

"With no money? With my father and his men bearing down on us? If it were only myself, then I would have left. But it was never only me. I think we were why my mother stayed, too." She swallowed hard. "And if she could do it for us, how could I do any less?"

"Your mother was good to you?"

"So good," Alessia said, remembering her beautiful, dark-haired mother, the gentle smile that had always put her at ease when her father was in the other room shouting. The sweet, soothing touch, a hand on her forehead to help her fall asleep. "I wanted to give them all what she gave to me. I was the oldest, the only one who remembered her very well. It seemed important I try to help them remember. That I give them the love I received, because I knew they would never get it from my father."

"And in New York? With me?"

"What do you mean?"

"You toed the line all of your life, Alessia. You were

prepared to marry to keep your brothers and sisters safe and cared for. Why did you even chance ruining it by sleeping with me?" His hold tightened on her, his voice getting back that rough edge. That genuine quality it had been missing since they'd stepped inside the hotel.

It was a good question. It was *the* question, really.

"Tell me, *cara*," he said, and she glimpsed something in his eyes as he spoke. A desperation.

And she couldn't goad him. Couldn't lie to him. Not now.

"Did you ever want something, Matteo, with all of yourself? So much that it seemed like it was in your blood? I did. For so many years. When we were children, I wanted to cross that wall between our families' estates and take your hand, make you run with me in the grass, make you smile. And when I got older…well, I wanted something different from you, starting about the time you rescued me, and I don't want to hear about how much you regret that. It mattered to me. I dreamed of what it would be like to kiss you, and then, I dreamed of what it would be like to make love with you. So much so that by the time I saw you in New York, when you finally did kiss me, I felt like I knew the steps to the dance. And following your lead seemed the easiest thing. How could I not follow?"

"I am a man, Alessia, so I fear there is very little romance to my version of your story. From the time you started to become a woman, I dreamed of your skin against mine. Of kissing you. Of being inside you. I could not have stopped myself that night any more than you could have."

"That's good to know," she said, heat rushing through her, settling over her skin. It made her dress, so lovely and formfitting a few moments ago, feel tight. Far too tight.

"I don't understand what it is you do to me."

"I thought… I was certain that I must not be so different from all your other women."

"There weren't that many," he said. "And you are different."

It was a balm to her soul that he felt that way. That she truly hadn't been simply one in a lineup. It was easy for her, she realized, to minimize the experience on his end. It had been easy for her to justify being with him, not being honest with him, giving him a one-night stand, because she'd assumed he'd had them before. It had been easy to believe she was the only one who'd stood to be hurt or affected, because she was the virgin.

That had been unfair. And she could see now, looking into his eyes, that it wasn't true, either.

"Kiss me," he said, all of the civility gone now.

She complied, closing the short distance between them, kissing him, really kissing him, for the first time in three months. Their wedding kiss had been nothing. A pale shadow of the passion they'd shared before. A mockery of the desire that was like a living beast inside of them both.

She parted her lips for him, sucked his tongue deep inside of her mouth, not caring that it would be obvious to the people around them. Matteo was hers now, her husband. She wouldn't hide it, not from anyone. Wouldn't hide her desire.

He growled low in his throat, the sound vibrating through his body. "Careful, Alessia, or I will not be responsible for what happens."

"I don't want you to be responsible," she said, kissing his neck. Biting him lightly. There was something happening to her, something that had happened once before. A total loss of control. At the hands of Matteo Corretti.

It was like she was possessed, possessed by the desire to have him, to take him, make him hers. Make him understand what she felt. Make herself understand what she felt.

"We can't do this here," he said.

"This sounds familiar."

"It does," he said. He shifted, pulled her away from his body, twining his fingers with hers. "Come with me."

"Where?"

"Somewhere," he said.

He led her out of the ballroom, ignoring everyone who tried to talk to them. A photographer followed them and Matteo cursed, leading them a different way, down a corridor and to the elevators.

He pushed the up button and they both waited. It only took a moment for the elevator doors to slide open, and the moment they did, she was being tugged inside, tugged up against the hard wall of his chest and kissed so hard, so deep, she was afraid she would drown in it.

She heard the doors slide closed behind them, was dimly aware of the elevator starting to move. Matteo shifted their positions, put her back up against the wall, his lips hungry on hers.

"I need you," he said, his voice shaking.

"I need *you*," she said.

Her entire body had gone liquid with desire, her need for him overshadowing everything. Common sense, self-protection, everything. There was no time for thought. This was Matteo. The man she wanted with everything she had in her, the man who haunted her dreams. This was her white knight, but he was different than she'd imagined.

There was a darkness to him. An edge she'd never been able to imagine. And she found she liked it. Found she wanted a taste of it. She didn't know what that said about her, didn't know what it meant, but at the moment, she didn't care, either.

"This is a beautiful dress," he said, tracing the deep V of the neckline with his fingertip, skimming silk and skin with the movement. Her breath hitched, her entire body on edge, waiting for what he would do next. Needing it more than she needed air. "But it is not as beautiful as you. And right now, I need to see you."

He reached around, tugging on the zipper, jerking it down.

"Careful," she said, choking on the word. "You'll snag the fabric."

"I'll tear it if I have to," he said.

The top fell around her waist, revealing her breasts, covered only by a whisper-thin bra that showed the outline of her nipples beneath the insubstantial fabric.

He lifted his hand and cupped her, slid his thumb over the tightened bud. "Hot for me?" he asked.

"Yes."

"Wet for me?" He put his other hand on her hip, flexed his fingers.

She couldn't speak, she just nodded. And he closed his eyes, his expression one of pained relief like she'd never seen before.

She put her hand between her breasts, flicked the front clasp on her bra, letting it fall to the elevator floor. He looked at her, lowering his head, sucking her deep into his mouth. An arrow of pleasure shot from there down to her core. She tightened her fingers in his hair, then suddenly became conscious of the continued movement of the elevator.

"Hit the stop button," she said, her voice breathless.

"What?" he asked, lifting his head, his cheeks flushed, his hair in disarray. Her heart nearly stopped. Matteo Corretti undone was the most amazing thing she'd ever seen.

"The elevator," she said.

He cursed and turned around, hitting the red button on the wall, the elevator coming to a halt. He cursed again and reached into his pocket, taking out his cell phone. "Just a second."

"You better not be texting," she said.

He pushed a few buttons, his eyes not straying to her. "Not exactly." He turned the screen toward her and she saw him. And her. And her breasts.

"Oh."

He pushed a few more buttons. "I have disabled the security camera now. Unless you like the idea of being on film."

She had to admit, she had a certain amount of curiosity as to what it looked like when Matteo Corretti made love to her. It was a video she wouldn't mind owning, in all honesty. But she didn't want it on security footage, either.

"Not in the mood to provide security with any early-evening jollies."

"No worries, I have now deleted that little stretch of footage. There are advantages to being a control freak. Having an app on your phone that lets you see all the security at your hotels, and do as you please with the cameras, is one of them."

He discarded his suit jacket and tie then, throwing them onto the floor of the elevator, tossing his phone down on top of them.

"Have you used that trick before?" she asked, before he lowered his head to kiss her again.

"With a woman?"

"Yes."

"Jealous?"

"Hell, yes," she said, not worried if he knew it. She wanted this moment, this desperation that was beyond anything she'd known, to be as foreign to him as it was to her.

"No, I haven't." He kissed her again, his tongue sliding against hers, and she forgot her lingering concerns.

Forgot about everything but what it felt like to have Matteo kissing her. Caressing her.

"Later—" he kissed the hollow of her throat "—I will do this right—" lowered his head and traced the line of her collarbone with his tongue. "I'll taste every inch of you. Take time to savor you. Take your clothes off slowly. Look at those gorgeous curves." He kissed her neck, bit her lightly like she'd done to him earlier. "Now, though... now I just need to be inside you."

He started to gather her skirt up in his hands, the slippery fabric sliding up her legs easily. "Take your panties off," he said.

She complied, her hands trembling as she worked her underwear down, kicking them to the side with her heels. He pushed her dress up around her hips, his hand hot on her thigh. He tugged her leg up around his, her back pinned against the wall of the elevator.

He tested her with his other hand, teasing her clitoris, sending streaks of white heat through her body with each pass his fingers made through her slick folds. "You didn't lie," he said. "You do want me."

"Yes," she said.

"Tell me," he said.

"I want you."

"My name."

"I want you, Matteo."

He abandoned her body for a moment, working at his belt, shoving his slacks and underwear down, just enough to free his erection so that he could sink into her. It was a shock, all those weeks without him, and she'd forgotten just how big he was. Just how much he filled her. She let her head fall back against the wall of the elevator, pleasure building deep inside her, her internal muscles tightening around his length.

And then there was no more talking. There was nothing but their ragged breathing, Matteo moving hard and fast inside her, blunt fingertips digging into her hips as he held her steady, thrusting into her.

He lowered his head, capturing her nipple in his mouth

again. A raw sound of pleasure escaped her lips and she didn't even care. She wasn't embarrassed at all.

Because this was Matteo. The man she'd always wanted. Wanted enough to break out of what was expected of her for the first time in her life. The man who had saved her, the man who made her angry and hurt her, the man who made her feel things she'd never felt before.

Matteo scared her. He confused her. He made her feel more than anyone else ever had.

And right now he was driving her to a point she'd never even imagined, to the edge of a cliff so high she couldn't see the bottom of the chasm below.

She was afraid to fall, afraid to let the pleasure that was building in her break, because she didn't know what would greet her on the other side. Didn't know what would happen. And something *would* happen. Something would change. There was no question. None at all.

And then he looked at her, those dark eyes meeting hers, and she saw him. Not the mask, the man. Raw need, desperation and a fear that mirrored her own.

He lowered his head, his lips pressing against her neck, his thrusts losing their measured rhythm. And something in her broke, released. And she was falling, falling into that endless chasm. But she wasn't afraid anymore.

Release rolled through her in waves, stealing every breath, every thought, everything but the moment.

And when she finally did reach bottom, Matteo was there, his strong arms around her. He was breathing hard, too, sweat on his brow, the back of his shirt damp, his heartbeat raging, so hard that, with his body pressed so tightly against hers, she could feel it against her own chest.

He stepped away from her slowly, running his hand over his hair, erasing the evidence that she'd ever speared her fingers through it. That she'd messed with his well-ordered control.

He adjusted his pants. Bent and collected his jacket, putting his phone back into his pocket. And she just stood there, her back to the wall, her dress still pushed partway up around her hips, the top resting at her waist, her underwear on the floor by her feet.

Matteo put his tie around his neck and started straightening it, too, before he looked at her. "Get dressed," he said.

"What?"

"Get dressed," he said. "We have to go back to the party."

"W-we do?"

"It's my charity," he said. "I have a speech to make." He checked his wristwatch. "And it seems I'm not too late for it so I really should try to manage it."

"I..."

"Turn around," he ordered, his voice harsh.

She did as he asked. He put her straps back into place, zipped the dress back up.

"My bra..."

"You don't need it," he said.

"What should I do with it?"

He opened up his jacket and indicated his inner pocket. She bent and scooped up her bra and panties and handed them to him, and he put both tiny garments into his pocket.

"Solved," he said.

She looked down at her chest, cupped her breasts for a moment. "I'm sagging."

"You are not."

He hit the button on the elevator and it started moving again, the doors sliding open. Then he hit the button for the first floor and they waited for the doors to close again.

Alessia felt...used. No, not even that. She just felt sad. Angry, because he was able to do that with her and then go back to his purely unruffled self.

Maybe she'd been making more out of them, and the sex, than she should have. Maybe she was wrong. Maybe it didn't mean anything to him. Nothing more than just sex, anyway, and a man like Matteo surely had it quite a bit.

They rode in silence, and the doors opened again. The photographer was still out there, wandering the halls. Looking for a photo op, no doubt.

Matteo put his arm around her waist and led her through the hall, that false smile back on his face. They started back toward the ballroom and she had the strangest feeling of déjà vu. Like they were back at the beginning of the night. Like their interlude in the elevator hadn't happened at all. But it had. She knew it had.

The photographer snapped a picture. And Alessia didn't bother to smile.

CHAPTER EIGHT

MATTEO WASN'T SURE how he managed to get up and speak in front of the large crowd of people. Not when he could see Alessia in the audience, her face smooth, serene, her dark eyes the only window to the storm that lurked beneath.

A storm he was certain would boil over and onto him once they were alone.

He found he didn't mind. That he welcomed the chance to take her on because it was better than the overwhelming, biting need to take her back to the elevator and have her again. To let the elevator continue up to his suite where he would have her again. And again. Tasting her this time, truly savoring her.

Yes, fighting was infinitely better than that. He would rather have her yelling at him than sighing his name in his ear.

Because he didn't know what to do with her, what to do about his desire for her.

It wasn't what he was used to. Wasn't normal in any way.

Sex was simply a need to be met, like eating or breathing. Yes, he liked some food better than he liked others, but he wasn't a slave to cravings. He believed in moderation, in exercising control in all areas of life.

Alessia was the one craving he didn't seem to be able to fight, and that meant he had to learn how.

Anything else was inexcusable.

"Thank you all for coming tonight, and for your generous donations. I am happy to announce that I am personally matching all of the donations given tonight. And that thanks to your generosity, it is now possible for the Corretti Education Foundation to branch out into college grants. It is my belief that a good education can overcome any circumstance, and it is my goal that every person be given that chance. Thank you again, enjoy the rest of the evening."

He stepped down from the podium, not paying attention to the applause that was offered up for his speech. He could hardly hear anything over the roar of blood in his ears. Could hardly see anything but Alessia. Which was one reason he allowed himself to be pulled to the side by some of the guests, interrupted on his way back to where his wife was standing.

He stopped and talked to everyone who approached him, using it as a tactic to keep himself from having to face Alessia without his guard firmly back in place. Cowardly? Perhaps. But he found he didn't care. Not much, at least.

Alessia didn't make a move to approach him; instead, she made conversation with the people around her. And every so often she flicked him a glare with those beautiful eyes of hers, eyes that glittered beneath the lights of the chandeliers. Eyes that made promises of sensual heaven, the kind of heaven he could hardly risk trying to enter again.

Every time he touched Alessia, she tore down another piece of the wall, that very necessary wall of control he'd built around himself.

People started to disperse, and as they both went along the natural line of people that wanted to converse with them, the space between them started to close. Matteo's blood started to flow hotter, faster, just getting nearer to Alessia.

No matter there were still five hundred people in the room. No matter that he'd had her against a wall an hour earlier. Still she challenged him. Still she made him react like a teenage boy with no control over his baser urges.

Yes, think about that. Remember what that looks like.

Blind rage. Two young men, still and unmoving, blood everywhere. And then a calm. A cold sort of emptiness. If he felt anything at all it was a kind of distant satisfaction.

And then he'd looked at Alessia. At the terror in her eyes.

And he'd done what he'd sworn he would never do.

He'd wrapped his arms around her and pulled her into his chest, brushing away her tears. He'd made her cry. Horrified her, and he couldn't blame her for being horrified. It wasn't the kind of thing a girl of fourteen, or any age, should ever have to see.

When he pulled away, when he looked down at her face, her cheeks were streaked with blood. The blood from his hands. Not the only blood he had on his hands.

He breathed in sharply, taking himself back to the present. Away from blood-soaked memories.

Except it was still so easy to see them when he looked at Alessia's face. A face that had been marred with tears and blood. Because of him.

The gap between them continued to shrink, the crowd thinning, until they met in the middle, in the same group. And there was no excuse now for him not to pull her against his side, his arm wrapped around her waist. So he did.

Alessia's body was stiff at his side, but her expression was still relaxed, her smile easy. A lie. Why had he never noticed before that Alessia's smile wasn't always genuine?

He'd assumed that it was. That Alessia displayed and felt emotion with ease and honesty. Now he wondered.

The last of the guests started to file out, leaving Alessia and Matteo standing in the empty ballroom.

He looked around, at the expansive room. This was his hotel, separate from his family dynasty, and often, looking at it, at the architecture, the expanse of it, filled him with a sense of pride. He had hotels all over the world, but this one, back in Sicily, a hotel that belonged to him and not to his family in any part, had always filled him with a particular amount of satisfaction.

Now it just seemed like a big empty room.

He picked up his phone and punched in a number. "Delay cleaning until further notice, I require the ballroom for personal use for a while."

Alessia looked at him, her dark eyes wide. "What do you need the ballroom for?"

He shrugged. "Anything I want." He walked over to the edge of the stage and sat, gripping the edge. "It is my hotel, after all."

"Yes, and you're a man who takes great pride in the ownership of whatever he can possess," she said.

"And why not?" he asked, loosening his tie, trying not to think of Alessia's fingers on the knot, trying not to imagine her fingers at the buttons of his dress shirt as he undid the collar. "That's what it's always been about in my family. I go out of town—" and off the grid "—and my bastard cousin has taken over my office. My younger brother has managed to charm his way into the top seat of the fashion houses for Corretti. So you see? In my family, ownership is everything. And if you have to stab someone to get it, all the better."

"Metaphorical stabbing?" she asked, wrapping her arms around her waist, as if holding herself together. He hated that. Hated that he might cause her pain in any way.

"Or literal stabbing. I told you, my family has a colorful history."

"You said you and your brothers weren't criminals."

"We're not. Not convicted, anyway," he added, not sure why. Maybe because, in his heart, he knew he was one.

Knew he could be convicted for assault several times over if evidence was brought before a court.

"Why are you saying this?"

"What do you mean, why am I saying this? I'm telling you the truth. Was what I did that day near your father's gardens legal? Answer me," he said, his words echoing in the empty room.

"You saved me."

"Maybe."

"They would have raped me," she said.

He remembered it so clearly. And yet so differently.

Because he remembered coming upon Alessia, backed up against a tree, a stone wall behind her, two men in front of her, pressing her back to the tree, touching her, jeering at her. They had her shirt torn. They were pushing her skirt up. And he'd known what they intended to do. The evil they meant for his angel.

And then he remembered seeing red.

He pushed off from the stage, standing and pacing, trying to relieve the restless energy moving through him. Trying to ease the tightness in his chest.

He hadn't simply stopped when he'd gotten those men away from Alessia. Hadn't stopped when they quit fighting back. He hadn't stopped until Alessia had touched his back. And then he'd turned, a rock held tightly in his hand, ready to finish what he'd started. Ready to make sure they never got up again, ready to make sure they could never hurt another woman again. Any other woman, but most especially Alessia.

But then he'd looked into her eyes. Seen the fear. Seen the tears.

And he'd dropped his hand back to his side, letting the rock fall to the ground. Letting the rage drain from his body.

That was when he'd realized what he had done. What he had been about to do. And what it had done to Alessia to see it. More than that, it confirmed what he'd always known. That if he ever let himself go, if he ever allowed himself more than his emotionless existence, he would become a man he hated.

"I did more than save you," he said. "A lot more."

"You did what you had to."

"You say it as if I gave it some thought. I didn't. What I did was a reaction. Blind rage. As I was, if you were not there, I wouldn't have ended it until they were dead."

"You don't know that."

"That's the thing, Alessia, I do know that. I know exactly what my next move was going to be, and trust me, it's not something people get back up from."

"I wish you could see what I saw."

"And I wish like hell you hadn't seen any of it," he said, his voice rough.

"You were…I thought…I thought they were going to get away with it. That no one would hear me scream. No one would stop them. I thought that they would do it. And then you came and you didn't let them. Do you have any idea what that meant to me? Do you know what you stopped?"

"I know what I stopped."

"Then why do you regret it so much?"

"I don't regret it, not like you mean." He could remember his father's face still, as he'd administered punishment to men in his debt. The calm. The absolute calm. But worse, he could remember his father's face when someone had enraged him. Could remember how volatile, how beyond reason, he became in those situations.

And always, the old man had a smug sense that he had done what must be done. Full and complete justification for every action.

Just as Matteo had felt after Alessia's attack. How he had felt after the fire.

"To me you were just a hero," she said, her words soft.

They hit him hard, like a bullet, twisted inside of him, blooming outward and touching him everywhere, scraping his heart, his lungs. For a moment, he couldn't breathe.

"It's so much more complicated than that," he said.

"Not to me. Not to the girl you rescued. You were like... You were every unfulfilled dream from my entire life, showing up when I needed you most. How can you not understand that?"

"Maybe that," he said, "is our problem now. You know a dream, a fantasy, and I am not that man. I'm not the hero of the story."

She shook her head. "You were the hero of my story that day. And nothing will change that."

Coldness invaded him. "Is that what led you to my bed that night?"

She didn't look away. "Yes."

He swore, the word loud in the empty expanse of the ballroom. "So that was my thank-you?"

"No!" she said, the exclamation reverberating around them. "It's not like that at all. Don't make it into something like that it's... No."

"Then what, Alessia? Your fantasy of a knight?" Her cheeks turned pink and then she did look away. "*Dio*, is that what it is? You expected me to be your chivalrous knight in shining armor? What a disappointment this must be for you. You would have likely been better off with Alessandro."

"I didn't want Alessandro."

"Only because you lied to yourself about who I am."

"Who are you, then?" she asked. "You're my husband. I think you should tell me."

"I thought we went over this already."

"Yeah, you gave me that internet bio of a rundown on who you are. We told each other things we already knew."

"Why do we have to know each other?"

"Because it seems like we should. We're...married."

"Not really."

"You took me into an elevator and had me against the wall—what would make it more real for you?" she asked, the words exploding from her, crude and true, and nothing he could deny.

"That's sex, Alessia, and what we have is great, explosive sex. But that kind of thing isn't sustainable. It's not meant to be. It's not good for it to be."

"And you know this because you're constantly having spontaneous, explosive sex with strangers?"

"No."

"Then how do you know?"

"There's no control in it. No sense. We nearly let it get filmed, nearly let the elevator go to the next floor. Neither of us think when sex is involved."

"Maybe you think too much."

"And maybe you don't think enough. You feel, and look where all of that feeling has gotten you."

Her lip curled into a sneer. "Don't you dare blame this on me! Don't you dare act like it was me and my girlish feelings that led us here. That's far too innocent of a take on it, first of all. Yes, I might have built you up as a hero in my head, but what I wanted that night in New York had nothing to do with you being some kind of paragon and everything to do with me wanting you as a woman wants a man. I didn't want hearts and flowers, I wanted sex. And that was what I got. That wasn't led by my feelings," she said, her words cold, "that was led by my body and I was quite happy with the results."

"Too bad the price was so steep."

"Wasn't it?"

Alessia looked at Matteo and, for a moment, she almost hated him. Because he was fighting so hard, against her, against everything. Or maybe she was the one fighting. And she was just mad at him for not being who she'd thought he was.

And that wasn't fair, not really. He couldn't help it if he didn't line up with the fantasy she'd created about him in her head. It wasn't even fair to expect him to come close.

But no one in her life had ever been there for her, not since her mother. It had all been about her giving. And then he'd been there, and he'd put it all on the line for her, he'd given her all of himself in that moment. And yes, what he'd done had been violent, and terrifying in a way, but it was hard for her to feel any sadness for the men who would have stolen her last bit of innocence from her.

She'd grown up in a house with a criminal father who lied and stole on a regular basis. She knew about the ugliness of life. She'd lost her mother, spent her days walking on eggshells to try to avoid incurring any of her father's wrath.

But in all that time, at least, no one had forced themselves on her sexually, and considering the kind of company her father kept, it had always seemed kind of an amazing thing.

And then someone had tried to take that from her, too. But Matteo had stopped it.

"Do you understand how much of my life has been decided for me?" she asked.

"Yes," he said slowly, obviously unwilling to admit to not understanding something.

"I don't think you do. I spent my days mothering my siblings, and I don't regret it, because it had to be done, but that meant I didn't go away to school. It meant I stayed at home when a lot of girls my age would have been moving out, going to university. I went to events my father wanted me to go to, hosted parties in dresses he deemed appropriate. That day...that day on the road, those two men tried to take another choice from me. They tried to choose how I would learn about sex, how I would be introduced to it. With violence and pain and force. They tried to take something from me, and I don't just mean virginity, I mean the way I saw myself. The way I saw men. The way I saw people. And you stopped them. So I'm sorry if you don't want to have been my hero, but you were. You let me hold on to some of my innocence. You let me keep some parts of life a fantasy. I know about how harsh life can be. I know about reality, but I don't need to have every horrible thing happen to me. And it was going to." Her voice was rough, raw with tears she needed to shed.

She turned away from him, trying to catch her breath.

"And then my father told me that I was going to marry Alessandro. And I could see more choices being taken from me but this time I didn't see a way out. Then my friend Carolina said she would host a bachelorette party for me. And for once my father didn't deny me. I didn't know you would be there. And Carolina suggested we go to your hotel and I...well, then I hoped you'd be there. And you were. And I saw another chance to make a choice. So don't ask me to regret it."

His eyes were black, endless, unreadable. "I won't ask you to regret it, because then I would have to regret it, and I don't. When I found out I was your first...I can't tell you how that satisfied me, and I don't care if that's not the done thing, if I shouldn't care, because I did. I still care. I'm still glad it was me."

"I am, too," she said, her voice a whisper. The honesty cost them both, she knew.

His eyes met hers, so bleak, so filled with need. And she hoped she could fill it. Hoped she could begin to understand the man that he was and not just the man she'd created a fiction about in her head.

She nearly went to him then. Nearly touched him. Asked him to lie her down on the cold marble of the ballroom floor and make love to her again. But then she remembered. Remembered the question he hadn't answered. The one she'd been determined to get the answer to before she ever let him touch her again.

She'd messed up earlier. She hadn't been able to think clearly enough to have a conversation with him. But now, she would ask now. Again. And she would get her answer.

"Will you be faithful to me?" she asked.

He pushed his fingers through his hair. "Why do you keep asking me this?"

"Because it's a simple question and one I deserve the answer to. I'm not sleeping with you if you won't promise I'm the only woman in your life."

"I can't love you," he said, the words pulled from him. Not *I don't love you*, like he'd said earlier, but *I can't.*

"I'm not asking you to love me, I'm asking you to not have sex with other women."

His jaw tightened, his hands clenching into fists at his sides. "To answer that question, I would have to know how I planned on conducting our relationship, and I do not know the answer to that yet."

"Were you planning on asking me?"

He shook his head. "I already told you we won't have a normal marriage."

"Why?" She knew she shouldn't ask, not in such a plaintive, needy tone, but she couldn't help herself, couldn't hide the hurt that was tearing through her. How was it she'd managed to get her dream, only to have it turn to ash the moment her fingers touched it?

"Because I cannot be a husband to you. I can't. I won't love you. I won't... I can't give what a husband is supposed to give. I don't know where to begin. I have an empire to run, my hotels, plus I have my bastard cousin installed in my offices at the family corporation, with his ass in my chair, sitting at my desk like he's the one who worked so hard for any of it. I don't have time to deal with you. If you took me on as a husband you would have me in your bed and nowhere else. And I'm not sure I want to put either of us through that."

"But you are my husband. Whether or not you want to be doesn't come into it at this point. You are my husband. You're the father of my baby."

"And our baby has the protection of my name, the validity of having married parents. I'm able to strike the deal for the docklands with your father thanks to this marriage and your siblings will be cared for. I'm sending them all to school, I don't think I told you."

Her throat closed, her body trembling. "I... No, you didn't."

"My point is, regardless of what happens behind closed doors, our marriage was a necessity, but what we choose to do in our own home rests squarely on us. And there are decisions to be made."

Decisions. She'd imagined that if she married Matteo her time for decision making would be over before it ever started. But he was telling her there was still a chance to make choices. That them legally being husband and wife didn't mean it was settled.

In some ways, the opportunity to make decisions was a heady rush of power she'd only experienced on a few occasions. In other ways...well, she wanted him to want to be married to her, if she was honest.

You're still chasing the fantasy when you have reality to contend with.

She had to stop that. She had to put it away now, the haze of fantasy. Had to stop trying to create a happy place where there wasn't one and simply stand up and face reality.

"So…if I say I don't want to be in a normal marriage, and if you can't commit to being faithful to me, does that mean that I have my choice of other lovers, too?"

Red streaked his cheekbones, his fists tightening further, a muscle in his jaw jerking. "Of course," he said, tight. Bitter.

"As long as there are no double standards," she said, keeping her words smooth and calm.

"If I release my hold on you, then I release it. We'll have to be discreet in public, naturally, but what happens behind closed doors is no one's business but our own."

"Ours and the elevator security cameras," she said.

"That will not happen again."

"It won't?"

"An unforgivable loss of control on my part."

"You've had a few of those recently."

She'd meant to spark an angry reply, to keep the fight going, because as long as they were fighting, she didn't ache for him. Wasn't so conscious of the tender emotions he made her feel. And she wasn't so overwhelmed by the need to be skin to skin to him when they were fighting. But she didn't get anger. Instead, she got a bleak kind of pain that echoed in her soul, a hopelessness in his dark eyes that shocked her.

"Yes," he said. "I have. Always with you."

"I don't know how you are in other areas of your life. I only know how you are with me," she said.

His eyes grew darker. "A pity for you. I'm much more pleasant than this, usually."

"I make you misbehave."

He chuckled, no humor in the sound. "You could say that. We should go home."

She nodded. "Yes, we should."

They were in an empty ballroom, and she really would have loved a romantic moment with him here. The chance to dance as the only two people in the room. To go up to his suite and make love. To share a moment with each other that was out of time, apart from reality.

But they'd had their fantasy. Reality was here now, well and truly.

She still didn't want to leave.

Matteo picked up his phone and dialed. "Yes, you can send in the crew now."

She swallowed hard, feeling like they'd missed a key moment. Feeling like she'd missed one.

"Let's go," he said. There was no press now, no one watching to see if he would put his arm around her. So he didn't. He turned and walked ahead, and she followed behind him, her heart sinking.

Matteo didn't know what he wanted. And she didn't, either.

No, that was a lie, she knew what she wanted. But it would require her to start dealing with Matteo as he was, and at some point, it would require him to meet her in the middle, it would require him to drop his guard.

She wasn't sure if either of them could do what needed to be done. Wasn't sure if they ever had a hope of fixing the tangled mess that they'd created.

She wasn't even sure if Matteo wanted to.

CHAPTER NINE

MATTEO WAS TEMPTED to drink again. He hated the temptation. He hated the feeling of temptation full stop. Before Alessia there had been no temptation.

No, that was a lie. The first temptation had been to break the rules and see what the Battaglias were really like. And so he had looked.

And from there, every temptation, every failing, had been tied to Alessia. She was his own personal road to ruin and there were some days he wondered why he bothered to stay off it.

At least he might go up in flames in her arms. At least then heat and fire might be connected with her, instead of that night his father had died.

Yes, he should just embrace it. He should just follow to road to hell and be done with it.

And bring her with you. Bring the baby with you.

Porca miseria. The baby.

He could scarcely think of the baby. He'd hardly had a moment. He felt a little like he was going crazy sometimes, in all honesty. There was everything that was happening with Corretti Enterprises, and he had to handle it. He should go in and try to wrench the reins back from Angelo, should kick Luca out of his position and expose whatever lie he'd told to get there because he was sure the feckless playboy hadn't gotten there on merit alone.

Instead, Matteo was tied up in knots over his wife. Bewitched by a dark-haired vixen who seemed to have him in a death grip.

She was the reason he'd left, the reason he'd gone up to a remote house he owned in Germany that no one knew about. The reason he hadn't answered calls or returned emails. The reason he hadn't known or cared he was being usurped in his position as head of his branch of the family business.

He had to get a handle on it, and he had no idea how. Not when he felt like he was breaking apart from the inside out.

The business stuff, the Corretti stuff, he could handle that. But he found he didn't care to, and that was the thing that got to him.

He didn't even want to think about the baby. But he had to. Didn't want to try to figure out what to do with Alessia, who was still sleeping in the guest bedroom in the palazzo, for heaven's sake.

Something had to be done. Action had to be taken, and for the first time in his life, he felt frozen.

He set his shot glass down on the counter and tilted it to the side before pushing the bottom back down onto the tile, the sound of glass on ceramic loud and decisive. He stalked out of the bar and into the corridor, taking a breath, trying to clear his head.

Alcohol was not the answer. A loss of control was not the answer.

He had to get a grip. On his thoughts. On his actions. He had a business to try to fix, deals to cement. And all he could think about was Alessia.

He turned and faced the window that looked out on the courtyard. Moonlight was spilling over the grass, a pale shade of gray in the darkness of night.

And then he saw a shadow step into the light. The brightness of the moon illuminated the figure's hair, wild and curling in the breeze. A diaphanous gown, so sheer the light penetrated it, showed the body beneath, swirled around her legs as she turned in a slow circle.

An angel.

And then he was walking, without even thinking, he was heading outside, out to the courtyard, out to the woman who woke something deep in his soul. Something he hadn't known existed before she'd come into his life.

Something he wished he'd never discovered.

But it was too late now.

He opened the back door and stepped out onto the terrace, walking to the balustrade and grasping the stone with his hands, leaning forward, his attention fixed on the beauty before him.

On Alessia.

She was in his system, beneath his skin. So deep he wondered if he could ever be free of her. It would be harder now, all things considered. She was his wife, the mother of his child.

He could send her to live in the *palazzolo* with his mother. Perhaps his mother would enjoy a grandchild.

He sighed and dismissed that idea almost the moment it hit. A grandchild would only make his mother feel old. And would quite possibly give her worry lines thanks to all the crying.

And you would send your child to live somewhere else?

Yes. He was considering it, in all honesty.

What did he know about children? What did he know about love? Giving it. Receiving it. The kind of nurturing, the father-son bond fostered by his father was one he would just as soon forget.

A bond forged, and ended, by fire.

He threw off the memories and started down the steps that led to the grass. His feet were bare and in that moment he realized he never went outside without his shoes.

A strange realization, but he became conscious of the fact when he felt the grass beneath his feet.

Alessia turned sharply, her dark hair cascading over her shoulder in waves. "Matteo."

"What are you doing out here?"

"I needed some air."

"You like being outdoors."

She nodded. "I always have. I hated being cooped up inside my father's house. I liked to take long walks in the sun, away from the...staleness of the estate."

"You used to walk by yourself a lot."

"I still do."

"Even after the attack?" The words escaped without his permission, but he found he couldn't be sorry he'd spoken them.

"Even then."

"How?" he asked, his voice rough. "How did you keep doing that? How did you go on as if nothing had changed?"

"Life is hard, Matteo. People you love die, I know you know about that. People who should love you don't treat you any better than they'd treat a piece of property they were trying to sell for a profit. I've just always tried to see the good parts of life, because what else could I do? I could sit and feel sorry for myself, but it wouldn't change anything. And I've made the choice to stay, so that would be silly. I made the choice to stay and be there for my brothers and sisters, and I can't regret it. That means I have to find happiness in it. And that means I can't cut out my walks just because a couple of horrible men tried to steal them from me."

"And it's that simple?"

"It's not simple at all, but I do it. Because I have to find a way to live my life. My life. It's the only one I have. And I've just learned to try to love it as it is."

"And do you?" he asked. "Do you love it?"

She shook her head. "No." Her voice was a whisper. "But I'm not unhappy all the time. And I think that's something. I mean, it has to count for something."

"What about now? With this?"

"Are you happy?"

"Happiness has never been one of my primary goals. I don't know that I've ever thought about it too closely."

"Everybody wants to be happy," she said.

Matteo put his hands into his pockets and looked over the big stone wall that partitioned his estate from the rest of the world, looked up at the moon. "I want to make something different out of my family. I want to do something more than threaten and terrorize the people in Palermo. Beyond that...does it matter?"

"It does matter. Your happiness matters."

"I haven't been unhappy," he said, and then he wondered if he was lying. "What about you, Alessia?"

"I made a decision, Matteo, and it landed me in a situation that hasn't been entirely comfortable. It was my first big mistake. My first big fallout. And no, not all of it has been happy. But I can't really regret it, either."

"I'm glad you don't regret me."

"Do you regret me?"

"I should. I should regret my loss of control more than I do—" a theme in his life, it seemed "—but I find I cannot."

"What about tonight? In the elevator? Why did you just walk away?"

"I don't know what to do with us," he said, telling the truth, the honest, raw truth.

"Why do we have to know what we're doing?"

"Because this isn't some casual affair, and it never can be." Because of how she made him feel, how she challenged him. But he wouldn't say that. His honesty had limits, and that was a truth he disliked admitting even to himself. "You're my wife. We're going to have a child."

"And if we don't try, then we're going to spend years sniping at each other and growing more and more bitter, is that better?"

"Better than hurting you? I think so."

"You've hurt me already."

"I did?"

"You won't promise to be faithful to me, you clearly hate admitting that you want me, even though as soon as we touch…Matteo, we catch fire, and you can't deny that. You know I don't have a lot of experience with men, but I know this isn't just normal. I know people don't just feel this way."

"And that's exactly why we have to be careful."

"So we'll be careful. But we're husband and wife, and I think we should try…try for the sake of our child, for our families, to make this marriage work. And I think we owe it to each other to not be unhappy."

"Alessia…"

"Let's keep taking walks, Matteo," she said, her voice husky. She took a step toward him, her hair shimmering in the dim light.

He caught her arm and pulled her in close, his heart pounding hard and fast. "I can't love you."

"You keep saying."

"You need to understand. There is a limit to what we can share. I'll have you in my bed, but that's as far as it goes. This wasn't my choice."

"I wasn't your choice?"

Her words hit him hard, and they hurt. Because no, he hadn't chosen to marry her without being forced into it. But it wasn't for lack of wanting her. If there was no family history. If he had not been the son of one of Sicily's most notorious crime bosses, if there was nothing but him and Alessia and every other woman on earth, he would choose her every time.

But he couldn't discount those things. He couldn't erase what was. He couldn't make his heart anything but cold, not just toward her, but toward anyone. And he couldn't afford to allow a change.

Alessia had no idea. Not of the real reasons why. Not the depth he was truly capable of sinking to. The man underneath the iron control was the very devil, as she had once accused him of being. There was no hero beneath his armor. Only ugliness and death. Only anger, rage, and the ability and willingness to mete out destruction and pain to those who got in his way.

If he had to choose between a life without feeling or embracing the darkness, he would take the blessed numbness every time.

"You know it wasn't."

She thrust her chin into the air. "And that's how you want to start? By reminding me you didn't choose me?"

"It isn't to hurt you, or even to say that I don't want you. But I would never have tied you to me if it wasn't a necessity, and that is not a commentary on you, but on me, and what I'm able to give. There are reasons I never intended to take a wife. I know who I am, but you don't."

"Show me," she said. And he could tell she meant it, with utter conviction. But she didn't know what she was asking. She had no way of knowing. He had given her a window into his soul, a glimpse of the monster that lurked beneath his skin, but she didn't know the half of it.

Didn't know what he was truly capable of. What his father had trained him for.

And what it had all led to seven years ago during the fire that had taken Benito's and Carlo's lives.

That was when he discovered that he truly was the man his father had set out to make him. That was when he'd discovered just how deep the chill went.

He was cold all the way down. And it was only control that held it all in check.

There was only one place he had heat. Only one way he could get warm. But it was a fine line, because he needed the cold. Needed his control, even with it...even with it he was capable of things most men would never entertain thoughts of. But without it he knew the monster would truly be unleashed. That it would consume him.

"I know what I'd like to show you," he said, taking a step toward her, putting his hand on her cheek. She warmed his palm. The heat, the life, that came from her, pouring into him. She shivered beneath his hand, as though his touch had frozen her, and he found it oddly appropriate.

If he kissed her, if he moved nearer to her now, he was making the choice to drag her into the darkness with him. To take what he wanted and use her to his own selfish ends.

He could walk away from her now and he could do the right thing. Protect her, protect their child. Give them both his name and a home, his money. Everything they would need.

She didn't need him in his bed, taking his pleasure in her body, using her to feel warm.

To court the fire and passion that could burn down every last shred of his control. It would be a tightrope walk. Trying to keep the lusts of his body from turning into a desire that overwhelmed his heart.

If he wanted Alessia, there was no other choice.

It was easy with her, to focus on his body. What he wanted from her. Because she called to him, reached him, made him burn in a way no other woman ever had.

With her, though, there was always something else. Something more.

He shut it down. Severed the link. Focused on his body. The burn in his chest, his gut. Everywhere. He was so hard it hurt. Hard with the need for her. To be in her. To taste her.

He could embrace that, and that only. And consign her to a life with a man who would never give her what she deserved.

In this case, he would embrace the coldness in him. Only an utter bastard would do this to her. So it was a good thing that was what he was.

He bent his head and pressed his lips to hers. It wasn't a deep kiss, it was a test. A test for him. To see if he could touch her without losing his mind.

She was soft. So soft. So alive. A taste of pure beauty in a world so filled with ugliness and filth. She reached into him and shone a light on him. On the darkest places in him.

No. He could not allow that. This was only about sex. Only about lust.

"Only me," she said when they parted.

"What?"

"You either have only me, or every other woman you might want, but before you kiss me again, Matteo, you have to make that decision."

His lips still tasted of her skin. "You." It was an easy answer, he found.

She put her hands on his face and drew up on her tiptoes. Her kiss was deep. Filled with the need and passion that echoed inside of his body. He wrapped his arm around her waist and relished every lush detail of holding her. Her soft curves, those generous breasts pressed against his chest. He slipped his hand over her bottom, squeezed her tightly. She was everything a woman should be. Total perfection.

She kissed his jaw, her lips light on his skin, hot and so very tempting. She made him want more, stripped him of his patience. He had always been a patient lover, the kind of lover who worked to ensure his partner's pleasure before taking his own. Because he could. Because even if he took pleasure with his body, his actions were dictated by his mind.

But she challenged that. Made him want so badly to lose himself. To think of nothing but her. Alessia. He was hungry for her in a way he had never hungered for anyone or anything.

He slid his hands over the bodice of her nightgown, cupped her breasts through the thin fabric and found she had nothing on underneath. He could feel her nipples, hard and scarcely veiled by the gauzy material.

He lowered his head and circled one of the tightened buds with his tongue, drew it deep into his mouth. It wasn't enough. He needed to taste her.

Her name pounded through his head in time with the beat of his heart. His need a living, breathing thing.

He gripped the straps of her gown and tugged hard, the top giving way. It fell around her waist, exposing her to him. He smoothed his hand over her bare skin, then lowered his head again, tasting her, filling himself with her.

He dropped to his knees and took the fabric in his hands, tugging it down the rest of the way, ignoring the sound of tearing fabric.

"I liked that nightgown," she said.

"It was beautiful." He kissed her stomach. "But it was not as beautiful as you are."

"You could have asked me to take it off."

"No time," he said, tracing a line from her belly button down to the edge of her panties. "I needed to taste you."

Her response was a strangled "Oh."

"Everywhere." He tugged at the sides of her underwear and drew them down her legs, tossing them to the side. He kissed her hip bone and she shuddered. "I think you should lay down for me, *cara*."

"Why is that?"

"All the better to taste you, *cara mia*."

"Can't you do it from where you are?"

"Not the way I want to."

She complied, her movements slow, shaky. It was a sharp reminder of how innocent she still was.

You let me hold on to some of my innocence.

Her words echoed in his mind as she sank to the ground in front of him, lying back, resting on her elbows, her legs bent at the knees.

No, he would not allow himself to be painted as some kind of hero. He might have saved her innocence then, but he had spent the past months ensuring that what remained was stripped from her. And tonight, he would continue it.

Keeping her bound to him would continue it.

It was too late to turn back now. Too late to stop. He put his hand on her thigh and parted her legs gently, sliding his fingers over the slickness at the entrance of her body. "Yes," he said, unable to hold the word back, a tremor of need racking his body.

He lowered his head to take in her sweetness, to try to satiate the need he felt for her. A need that seemed to flow through his veins along with his blood, until he couldn't tell which one was sustaining him. Until he was sure he needed both to continue breathing.

He was lost in Alessia. Her flavor, her scent.

He pushed one finger deep inside her while he continued to lavish attention on her with his lips and tongue. She arched up against him, a raw cry escaping her lips. And he took it as her approval, making his strokes with mouth and hands firmer, more insistent.

She drove her fingers deep into his hair, tugging hard, the pain giving him the slight distraction he needed to continue. Helping him hold back his own need.

He slipped a second finger inside of her and her muscles pulsed around him, her body getting stiff beneath him, her sound of completion loud, desperate. Satisfying to him on a level so deep he didn't want to examine it too closely.

He didn't have time to examine it because now he needed her. Needed his own release, a ferocity that had him shaking. He rose up, pausing to kiss her breasts again, before taking possession of her mouth.

He sat up and tugged his shirt over his head, shrugging his slacks down as quickly as possible, freeing his aching erection.

"Are you ready?" he asked. He needed the answer to be yes.

"Yes."

He looked at her face, at Alessia, and as he did, he pushed inside the tight heat of her body. He nearly lost it then, a cold sweat breaking out over his skin, his muscles tense, pain coursing through him, everything in him trying to hold back. To make this last.

"Matteo."

It was her voice that broke him. Her name on his lips. He started to thrust hard into her, and no matter how he told himself to take it slow, take it gentle, he couldn't. He was a slave to her, to his need.

Finesse was lost. Control was lost.

She arched against him every time he slid home, a small sigh of pleasure on her lips. He lowered his head, buried his face in her neck, breathing her in. Lilacs and skin. And the one woman he would always know. The one woman who mattered.

Sharp nails dug into the flesh on his shoulder, but this time, the pain didn't bring him back. He lost himself, let his orgasm take him over, a rush of completion that took him under completely. He was lost in a wave, and burning. Burning hot and bright, nothing coming to put him out. To give him any relief. All he could do was hang on and weather it. Try to survive a pleasure so intense it bordered on destructive.

And when it was over, she was there, soft arms wrapped around him, her scent surrounding him.

"Will it always be like this?" Alessia's voice was broken with sharp, hard breaths.

He didn't have an answer for her. He couldn't speak. Couldn't think. And he hoped to God it wouldn't always be like this because there was no way his control could withstand it. And at the same time he knew he couldn't live with her and deny himself her body.

He would keep it under control. He would keep his heart separate from his body. He'd done it with women all his life. He'd done it when his father had asked him to learn the family business. The night his father had forced him to dole out punishment to a man in debt to the Corretti family.

He had locked his heart in ice and kept himself from feeling. His actions unconnected to anything but his mind.

He could do it again. He would.

"We should go inside," he said, sitting up, his breathing still ragged.

"Yeah. I'm pretty sure I have grass stains in…places."

He turned to her, a shocked laugh bursting from him. A real laugh. He couldn't remember the last time he'd laughed and meant it. "Well, you should be glad I made quick work of your gown, then."

"You tore it," she said, moving into a standing position and picking up her shredded garment.

"You liked it."

He could see her smile, even in the dim light. "A little."

There was a strange lightness in his chest now, a feeling that was completely foreign to him. As though a rock had been taken off his shoulders.

"I'm hungry," she said.

She started walking back toward the house, and he kept

his eyes trained on her bare backside, on the twin dimples low on her back. She was so sexy he was hard again already.

He bent and picked his underwear up from the ground, tugging the black boxer briefs on quickly and following her inside. "Do you want to eat?" he asked.

"Yes, I do." She wandered through the maze of rooms, still naked, and he followed.

"And what would you like?"

"Pasta. Have you got an apron?"

"Have I got an apron?"

"You have a cook, yes?"

"Yes."

"Does he have an apron?"

"She." He opened the pantry door and pulled a short red apron off a hook.

Alessia smiled and slipped the apron over her head, tying it tight. She was a lot taller than the little round woman he'd hired to cook his meals. The apron came down just to the tops of her thighs and it tied in the back, exposing her body to him from that angle.

"Dinner and a show," he said.

She tossed him a playful glare, then started riffling through the cabinets. "What kind of pasta have you got?"

"Fresh in the fridge," he said.

She opened up the stainless-steel fridge and bent down, searching for a few moments before popping up with a container that held pappardelle pasta and another that had marinara sauce.

She put a pan of water on the stove, then put the sauce in another pan to reheat, and leaned back against the counter, her arms crossed beneath her breasts.

"Didn't you ever hear that a watched pot never boils?"

"No. Who says that?"

"People do," he said.

"Did your mom say it to you?"

"No. A cook we had, I think."

"Oh. It's the kind of thing my mother probably would have said to me someday. If she had lived."

"You miss her still."

"I always will. But you lost your father."

Guilt, ugly, strangling guilt, tightened in his chest. "Yes."

"So you understand."

He shook his head slowly. "I'm not sure I do."

"You don't miss him?"

"Never."

"I know your father was hard to deal with. I know he was…I know he was shady like my father but surely you must—"

"No," he said.

"Oh."

"Will you miss your father?"

"I think so. He's not a wonderful man, but he's the only father I have."

"I would have been better off without one than the one that I had."

Alessia moved to put the pasta into the pan. "You say that with a lot of certainty."

"Trust me on this, Alessia."

They stood in silence until the pasta was done. Matteo got bowls out of the cupboard and set them on the counter and Alessia dished them both a bowl of noodles and sauce.

"Nothing like a little post…you know, snack," she said, lifting her bowl to her lips, her eyes glued to his chest. "You're barely dressed."

"You should talk," he said.

She looked down. "I'm dressed."

"Turn around." She complied, flashing her bare butt to him. "That's not dressed, my darling wife."

"Are you issuing a formal complaint?"

"Not in the least. I prefer you this way."

"Well, the apron is practical. Don't go tearing it off me if you get all impatient." She took a bit of pasta and smiled, her grin slightly impish. It made it hard to breathe.

There was something so normal about this. But it wasn't a kind of normal he knew. Not the kind he'd ever known. He wasn't the sort of man who walked barefoot in the grass and then ate pasta at midnight in his underwear.

He'd never had a chance to be that man. He wondered again at what it would be like if all the things of the world could simply fall away.

"Matteo?"

"Yes?"

"I lost you for a second. Where were you?"

"Just thinking."

"Mmm." She nodded. "I'm tempted to ask you what about but I sort of doubt you'd want to tell me."

"About my father," he said, before he could stop himself.

"You really don't miss him?"

"No." A wall of flame filled his mind. An image of the warehouse, burning. "Never."

"My father has mainly ignored my existence. The only time he's ever really acknowledged me is if he needs something, or if he's angry."

Rage churned in Matteo's stomach. "Did he hit you?"

"Yes. Not beatings or anything, but if I said something that displeased him, he would slap my face."

"He should feel very fortunate he never did so in front of me."

Alessia was surprised at the sudden change in Matteo's demeanor. At the ice in his tone. For a moment, they'd actually been getting along. For a moment, they'd been connecting with clothes on, and that was a rarity for the two of them.

He was willing to try. He'd told her that. And he would be faithful. Those were the only two promises she required from him. Beyond that, she was willing to take her chances.

Willing to try to know the man she'd married. Past her fantasy of him as a hero, as her white knight, and as the man he truly was. No matter what that might mean.

"I handled it," she said.

"It was wrong of him."

She nodded. "I know. But I was able to keep him from ever hitting one of the other kids and that just reinforced why I was there. Yes, I bore the brunt of a lot of it. I had to plan parties and play hostess, I had to take the wrath. But I've been given praise, too."

"I was given praise by my father sometimes, too," Matteo said. There was a flatness to his tone, a darkness in his words that made her feel cold. "He spent some time, when I was a bit older, teaching me how to do business like a Corretti. Not the business we presented to the world. The clean, smooth front. Hotels, fashion houses. All of that was a cover then. A successful cover in its own right, but it wasn't the main source of industry for our family."

"I think…I mean, I think everyone knows that."

"Yes, I'm sure they do. But do you have any idea how far-reaching it was? How much power my father possessed? How he chose to exercise it?"

She shook her head, a sick weight settling in her stomach. "What did he do, Matteo? What did he do to you?"

"To me? Nothing. In the sense that he never physically harmed me."

"There are other kinds of harm."

"Remember I told you I wasn't a criminal? That's on a technicality. It's only because I was never convicted of my crimes."

"What did he do to you, Matteo?" Her stomach felt sick now, and she pushed her bowl of food across the counter, making her way to where Matteo was standing.

"When I was fifteen he started showing me the ropes. The way things worked. He took me on collection calls. We went to visit people who owed him money. Now, my father was only ever involved on the calls where people owed him a lot of money. People who were in serious trouble with him. Otherwise, his men, his hired thugs, paid the visits."

"And he took you on these...visits?"

Matteo nodded, his arms crossed over his bare chest. There was a blankness in his eyes that hurt, a total detachment that froze her inside.

"For the first few weeks I just got to watch. One quick hit to the legs. A warning. A bone-breaking warning, but much better than the kind of thing he and his thugs were willing to do."

"*Dio.* You should never have... He should never have let you see..." She stopped talking then, because she knew there was more. And that it was worse. She could feel the anxiety coming off him in waves.

She took a step toward him, put her hand on his forearm. It was damp with sweat, his muscles shaking beneath her touch.

"One night he asked me to do it," he said.

His words were heavy in the room, heavy on her. They settled over her skin, coating her, making her feel what he felt. Dirty. Ashamed. She didn't know how she was so certain that was what he felt, but she was.

"What happened?" She tried to keep her voice steady, tried to sound ready to hear it. Tried to be ready to hear it. Because he needed to say it without fear of recrimination from her. Without fear of being told there was something wrong with him.

She knew that as deeply, as innately, as she knew his other feelings.

"I did it," he said. "My father asked me to break a man's legs because he owed the family money. And I did."

CHAPTER TEN

MATTEO WAITED FOR the horror of his admission to sink in. Waited for Alessia to turn from him, to run away in utter terror and disgust. She should. He wouldn't blame her.

He also desperately wanted her to stay.

"Matteo…"

"These hands," he said, holding them out, palms up, "that have touched you, have been used in ways that a man should never use his hands."

"But you aren't like that."

He shook his head. "Clearly I am."

"But you didn't enjoy it."

"No. I didn't enjoy it." He could remember very vividly how it had felt, how the sweat had broken out on his skin. How he had vomited after. His father's men had found that terribly amusing. "But I did it."

"What would your father have done to you if you hadn't?"

He shook his head. "It doesn't matter."

"Yes, it does, Matteo, you were a boy."

"I was a boy, but I was old enough to know that what my father did, what he was, was wrong."

"And you were trapped in it."

"Maybe. And maybe that would be an acceptable excuse for some people, but it's not for me."

"Why not? You were a boy and he abused you. Tell me,

and be honest, what did he say he would do to you if you didn't do it?"

Matteo was afraid for one moment that his stomach might rebel against him. "He told me if I couldn't do it to a grown man, there were some children in the village I might practice on."

Alessia's face contorted with utter horror. "Would he have done that?"

"I don't know. But I wasn't going to find out, either."

"He made you do it."

"He manipulated me into doing it, but I did it."

"How?" she asked, her voice a whisper.

"It's easy to do things, anything, when you can shut the emotion down inside yourself. I learned to do that. I learned that there was a place inside of myself as cold as any part of my father's soul. If I went there, it wasn't so hard to do." It was only after that he had broken. In the end, it was both the brokenness, and the cold, that had saved him.

His father had decided he wasn't ready. Didn't want his oldest son, the one poised to take over his empire, undermining his position by showing such weakness.

And after, the way he'd dealt with the knowledge that he'd lived with a monster, the way he'd dealt with knowing that he was capable of the very same atrocities, was to freeze out every emotion. He would not allow himself to want, to crave power or money in the way his father did. Passion, need, greed, were the enemy.

Then he'd seen Alessia. And he had allowed her a place inside him, a place that was warm and bright, one that he could retreat to. He saw happiness through her eyes when he watched her. His attraction to her not physical, but emotional. He let a part of himself live through her.

And that day when he'd seen those men attacking her, the monster inside him had met up against passion that had still existed in the depths of him, and had combined to create a violence that was beyond his control. One that frightened him much more than that moment of controlled violence in his father's presence had.

More even than that final act, the one that had removed his father from his life forever.

Because it had been a choice he'd made. It had been fueled by his emotion, by his rage, and no matter how deserving those men had been…it was what it said about himself that made him even more certain that it must never happen again. That he must never be allowed to feel like that.

"Do you see?" he asked. "Do you see what kind of man I am?"

She nodded slowly. "Yes. You're a good man, with a tragic past. And the things that happened weren't your fault."

"When I went back home the day of your attack, there was still blood all over me. I walked in, and my father was there. He looked at me, saw the evidence of what had happened. Then he smiled, and he laughed," Matteo spat. "And he said to me, 'Looks like you're ready now. I always knew you were my son.'"

That moment was burned into his brain, etched into his chest. Standing there, shell-shocked by what had happened, by what he had done. By what had nearly happened to Alessia. And having his father act as though he'd made some sort of grand passage into manhood. Having him be proud.

"He was wrong, Matteo, you aren't like him. You were protecting me, you weren't trying to extort money out of those men. It's not the same thing."

"But it's the evidence of what I'm capable of. My father had absolute conviction in what he did. He could justify it. He believed he was right, Alessia, do you understand that? He believed with conviction that he had a right to this money, that he had the right to harm those who didn't pay what he felt he was owed. All it takes is a twist of a man's convictions."

"But yours wouldn't be..."

"They wouldn't be?" He almost told her then, but he couldn't. The words he could never say out loud. The memory he barely allowed himself to have. "You honestly believe that? Everyone is corruptible, *cara*. The only way around it is to use your head, to learn what is right, and to never ever let your desire change wrong to right in your mind. Because that's what desire does. My father's desire for money, your father's desire for power, made them men who will do whatever it takes to have those things. Regardless of who they hurt. And I will never be that man."

"You aren't that man. You acted to save me, and you did it without thought to your own safety. Can't you see how good that is? How important?"

"I don't regret what I did," he said, choosing his words carefully. "I had a good reason to do it. But how many more good reasons could I find? If it suited me, if I was so immersed in my own needs, in my own desires, what else might I consider a good reason? So easily, Alessia, I could be like Benito was."

"No, that isn't true."

"Why do you think that?"

"Because you're...good."

He laughed. "You are so certain?"

"Yes. Yes, Matteo, I'm certain you're good. Do you know what I remember from that day? The way you held me after. Do you know how long it had been since someone had tried to comfort me? Since someone had wiped away my tears? Not since my mother. Before that, I had done all of the comforting, and then when I needed someone? You were there. And you told me it would be okay.

More than that, you made it okay. So don't tell me you aren't good. You are."

He didn't believe her, because she didn't know the whole truth. But he wanted to hold her words tightly inside of him, wanted to cling to her vision of him, didn't want her to see him any other way.

"I got blood on your face," he said, his voice rough. "That day when I wiped your tears."

She looked at him with those dark, beautiful eyes. "It was worth it." She took a step toward him, taking his hand in hers. "Come on. Let's go to bed."

And he was powerless to do anything but follow her.

Alessia woke the next morning with a bone-deep feeling of contentment. She noticed because she'd never felt anything like it before. Had never felt like things were simply right in the world. That there wasn't anything big left to accomplish. That she just wanted to stay and live in the moment. A moment made sweeter by the fact that there was nothing pressing or horrible looming in the future.

Then she became conscious of a solid, warm weight at her back, a hand resting on her bare hip. And she was naked, which was unusual because she normally slept in a nightgown.

A nightgown that was torn.

A smile stretched across her face and she rolled over to face Matteo. Her lover. Her husband. He was still sleeping, the lines on his forehead smoothed, his expression much more relaxed than it ever was when he was awake.

She leaned over and kissed his cheek, the edge of his mouth. She wanted him again. It didn't matter how many times he'd turned to her in the middle of the night, she wanted him again. It didn't matter if they had sex, or if he just touched her, but she wanted him. His presence, his kiss, him breathing near her.

This moment was one she'd dreamed of for half of her life. This moment with Matteo Corretti. Not with any other man.

She'd woken up next to him once before, but she hadn't been able to savor it. Her wedding had been looming in the not-too-distant future and guilt and fear had had her running out the door before Matteo had woken up.

But not this morning. This morning, she would stay with him until he woke. And maybe she would share his bed again tonight. And every night after that. He was her husband, after all, and it only seemed right that they sleep together.

They were going to try to make a real marriage out of a legal one.

He'll never love you.

She ignored the chill that spread through her veins when that thought invaded her mind. It didn't matter. She wouldn't dwell on it. Right now, she had a hope at a future she could be happy with. Matteo in her bed. In her life.

And she was having his baby. At some point, that would sink in and not just be a vague, sort of frightening, sort of wonderful thought.

But right now, she was simply lingering in the moment. Not wondering if Matteo's feelings would ever change, not worrying about changing diapers.

He shifted then, his eyes fluttering open. "Good morning," he said. So much different than his greeting the morning after their wedding.

"Good morning, handsome."

"Handsome?"

"You are. And I've always wanted to say that." *To you.*

"Alessia...you are something."

"I know, right?" Matteo rolled over onto his back and she followed him, resting her breasts on his chest, her chin propped up on her hands. "Last night was wonderful."

He looked slightly uncomfortable. Well, she imagined she wasn't playing the part of blasé sophisticate very well, but in her defense…she wasn't one. She was a woman with very little sexual experience having the time of her life with a man who'd spent years as the star attraction in her fantasies. It was sort of hard to be cool in those circumstances.

He kissed her, cupping her chin with his thumb and forefinger. She closed her eyes and hummed low in her throat. "You're so good at that," she said when they parted. "I feel like I have a post-orgasm buzz. Is that a thing?"

He rolled onto his side again and moved into a sitting position, not bothering to cover himself with the blankets.

"I don't know," he said. "I can't say I've ever experienced it."

"Oh." That hurt more than it should have. Not because she wanted him to have experienced post-orgasm buzz with anyone else, but because she wished he'd experienced it with her.

"What is it, *cara*?"

"Nothing." She put her palm flat on his chest and leaned in, her lips a whisper from his. Then his phone started vibrating on the nightstand.

"I have to take that," he said, moving away from her. He turned away from her and picked it up. "Corretti." Every muscle in his back went rigid. "What the hell do you want, Alessandro?"

Alessia's stomach rolled. Alessandro. She would rather not think about him right at the moment. She felt bad for the way things had ended. He'd been nice enough to her, distant, and there had been no attraction, but he'd been decent. And she'd sort of waited until the last minute to change her mind.

She got out of bed and started hunting for some clothes.

There was nothing. Only a discarded red apron that she knew from last night didn't cover a whole lot.

"I'm busy, you can't just call a meeting and expect me to drop everything and come to you like a lapdog. Maybe you're used to your family treating you that way, but you don't get that deference from me."

Alessia picked the apron up and put it on. It was better than nothing.

Matteo stood from the bed, completely naked, pacing the room. She stood for a moment and just watched. The play of his muscles beneath sleek, olive skin was about the sexiest thing she'd ever seen.

"Angelo?" The name came out like a curse. "What are you doing meeting with that bastard?" A pause. "It was a commentary on his character, not his birth. Fine. Noon. Salvatore's."

He pushed the end-call button and tossed the phone down on the bed, continuing to prowl the room. "That was Alessandro."

"I got that."

"He wants me to come to a meeting at our grandfather's. With Angelo, of all people."

"He's your cousin. He's family, and so is Alessandro."

"I have enough family that I don't like. Why would I add any more?"

"You don't even like your brothers?"

"No."

"Why don't you like your brothers?"

"Because if I ever do seem to be in danger of being sucked into the Corretti mind-set it's when we start playing stupid business games."

"But they're your family."

"My family is a joke. We're nothing but criminals and selfish assholes who would sell each other out for the right price. And we've all done it."

"So maybe someone needs to stop," she said, her voice soft.

"I don't know if we can."

"Maybe you should be the first one?"

"Alessia…"

"Look, I know I'm not a business mind, and I know I don't understand the dynamics of your family, but if you hate this part of it so much, then end it."

"I need to get dressed."

"I'll go make breakfast," she said. "I'm dressed for it."

"You might give my staff a shock."

"Oh—" her cheeks heated "—right, on second thought I might go back to my room."

"That's fine. And after that, you can ask Giancarlo if he would have your things moved into the master suite."

"You want me to move in?"

"Yes. You tramping back to your room in an apron is going to get inconvenient quickly, don't you think?"

Alessia felt her little glow of hope grow. "Yeah. Definitely it would be a little bit inconvenient. I would love to move into your room."

"Good." He leaned in and dropped a kiss on her lips. "Now, I have to get ready."

When Salvatore had been alive, Matteo had avoided going to his grandparents' home as often as he could. The old man was a manipulator and Matteo was rarely in the mood for his kind of mind games.

Still, whenever his grandmother had needed him, he had been there. They all had. This had long been neutral ground for that very reason. For Teresa. Which made it a fitting setting for what they were doing today.

Matteo walked over the threshold and was ushered back toward the study. He didn't see his grandmother, or any of the staff. Only a hostile-looking Alessandro, and Angelo sitting in a chair, a drink in hand.

"What was so important that you needed to speak to me?"

"Sorry to interrupt the blissful honeymoon stage with your new bride. I assume she actually went through with your wedding," Alessandro said.

"She did," he said.

Angelo leaned back in one of the high-backed chairs, scanning the room. "So this is what old Corretti money buys. I think I prefer my homes."

"We all prefer not to be here," Matteo said. "Which begs the question again, why are we?"

"You married Alessia, I can only assume that means you've cut a deal with her father?"

"Trade in and out of Sicily is secured for the Correttis and the docklands are ours. The revitalization project is set to move forward."

"Handy," Angelo said, leaning forward, "because I secured a deal with Battaglia, as well." Angelo explained the details of the housing development he was working on, eased by Battaglia's connections.

"And what does that have to do with us?"

"Well," Angelo continued, "it can have a lot to do with you. Assuming you want to take steps to unify the company."

"We need to unify," Alessandro said, his tone uncompromising. "Otherwise, we'll just spend the next forty years tearing everything apart. Like our fathers did."

Matteo laughed, a black, humorless sound. "You are my cousin, Alessandro, but I have no desire to die in a warehouse fire with you."

"That's why this has to end," Alessandro said. "I have a proposal to make. One that will see everyone in the family with an equal share of power. It will put us in the position to make the company, the family, strong again. Without stooping to criminal activity to accomplish it."

Alessandro outlined his plan. It would involve everyone, including their sisters, giving everyone equal share in the company and unifying both sides for the first time.

"This will work as long as this jackass is willing to put some of the extra shares he's acquired back into the pot," Alessandro said, indicating Angelo.

"I said I would," Angelo responded, his acquiescence surprising. Equally surprising was the lack of venom and anger coming from the other man. Or maybe not. Matteo had to wonder if Angelo had met a woman. He knew just the kind of change a woman could effect on a man.

"There you are," Alessandro said. "Are you with us?"

Matteo thought of the fire. Of the last time he'd seen his father. Of all that greed had cost. This was his chance to put an end to that. To start fresh. The past could never be erased, it would always be there. But the future could be new. For him. For Alessia. For their child.

He had too many other things in his life, good things, to waste any effort holding on to hatred he didn't even have the energy to feel.

He extended his hand and Alessandro took it, shaking it firmly. Then Matteo extended his hand to Angelo and, for the first time, shook his hand. "I guess that means you're one of us now," he said to Angelo. "I don't know if you should be happy about that or not."

"I'll let you know," Angelo said. "But so far, it doesn't seem so bad."

"All right, where do I sign?"

CHAPTER ELEVEN

MATTEO WAS EXHAUSTED by the time he got around to driving back to his palazzo. Dealing with Alessandro, going to his grandfather's house, had been draining in a way he had not anticipated. And yet, in some ways, there was a weight lifted. The promise of a future that held peace instead of violence. The first time his future had ever looked that way.

And he had Alessia to go home to. That thought sent a kick of adrenaline through him, made him feel like there was warmth in his chest. Made him feel like he wasn't so cold.

He left the car parked in front of his house with the keys in the ignition. One of his staff would park it for him later. And if not, he didn't mind it being there in the morning. But he couldn't put off seeing Alessia, not for another moment. He needed to see her for some reason, needed affirmation of who he was. To see her face light up. To have someone look at him like they didn't know who and what he was.

Alessandro and Angelo didn't know about his past, but they knew enough about the family to have an idea. Alessandro certainly hadn't escaped a childhood with Carlo without gaining a few scars of his own.

But Alessia looked at him like none of that mattered. Like she didn't know or believe any of it.

That isn't fair. She should know.

No, he didn't want her to know. He wanted to keep being her knight. To have one person look and see the man he might have been if it weren't for Benito Corretti.

He would change what it meant to be a Corretti for his child. He would never let them see the darkness. Never.

A fierce protectiveness surged through him, for the first time a true understanding of what it meant for Alessia to be pregnant.

A child. His child.

He prowled through the halls of the palazzo and found Alessia in a sitting room, a book in her hands, her knees drawn up to her chest. She was wearing a simple sundress that had slid high up her thighs. He wanted nothing more than to push it up the rest of the way, but he also found he didn't want to disturb her. He simply wanted to look.

She raised her focus then, and her entire countenance changed, her face catching the sunlight filtering through the window. Her dark eyes glittered, her smile bright. Had anyone else ever looked at him like that?

He didn't think they had.

"How did the meeting go?"

"We called each other names. Insulted each other's honor and then shook hands. So about as expected."

She laughed. "Good, I guess."

"Yes. We've come up with a way to divide Corretti Enterprises up evenly. A way for everyone to get their share. It's in everyone's best interests, really. Especially the generation that comes after us. Which I now have a vested interest in."

She smiled, the dimple on her left cheek deepening. "I suppose you do. And...I'm glad you do."

He moved to sit on the couch, at her feet, then he leaned in. "Can you feel the baby move yet?"

She shook her head. "No. The doctor said it will feel like a flutter, though."

"May I?" he asked, stretching his hand out, just over the small, rounded swell of her stomach.

"Of course."

He swallowed hard and placed his palm flat on her belly. It was the smallest little bump, but it was different than it had been. Evidence of the life that was growing inside her. A life they'd created.

She was going to be the mother of his child. She deserved to know. To really understand him. Not to simply look at him and see an illusion. He'd given her a taste of it earlier, but his need for that look, that one she reserved just for him, that look he only got from her, had prevented him from being honest. Had made him hold back the most essential piece of just why he was not the man to be her husband.

The depth to which he was capable of stooping.

Because no matter how bright the future had become, the past was still filled with shadows. And until they were brought into the sunlight, their power would remain.

"There is something else," he said, taking his hand from her stomach, curling it into a fist. His skin burned.

"About the meeting?"

"No," he said. "Not about the meeting."

"What about?"

"About me. About why…about why it might not be the best idea for you to try to make a marriage with me. About the limit of what I can give."

"Matteo, I already told you how I feel about what happened with your father."

"By that you mean when he took me on errands?"

"Well…yes."

"So, you don't mean what happened the night of the warehouse fire that killed him and Carlo."

"No. No one knows what happened that night."

"That isn't true," he said, the words scraping his throat raw. "Someone knows."

"Who?" she asked, but he could tell she already knew.

"I know."

"How?"

"Because, *cara mia*, I was there."

"You were there?"

He nodded slowly. Visions of fire filled his mind. Fire and brimstone, such an appropriate vision. "Yes. I was there to try to convince my father to turn over the holdings of Corretti to me entirely. I wanted to change things. To end the extortion and scams. All of it. But he wouldn't hear it. You see, at the time, he was still running criminal schemes, using the hotels, which I was managing, to help launder money. To help get counterfeit bills into circulation, into the right hands. Or wrong hands as the case may have been. I didn't want any part of it, but as long as my father was involved in the running of the corporation, that was never going to end. I wanted out."

"Oh," Alessia said, the word a whisper, as if she knew what was coming next. He didn't want her to guess at it, because he wanted, perversely, for her to believe it impossible. For her to cling to the white-knight image and turn away from the truth he was about to show her.

"I don't know how the fire started. But the warehouse was filled with counterfeiting plates, and their printing presses. That's one way to make money, right? Print your own."

He looked down at his hands, his heart pounding hard, his stomach so tight he could hardly breathe. "The fire spread quickly. I don't know where Carlo was when it broke out. But I was outside arguing with my father. And he turned and…and he looked at the blaze and he started to walk toward it."

Matteo closed his eyes, the impression of flames burning bright behind his eyelids. "I told him if he went back into that damned warehouse to rescue those plates, I would leave him to it. I told him to let it burn. To let us start over. I told him that if he went back, I would be happy to let him burn with it all, and then let him continue to burn in hell."

"Matteo...no." She shook her head, those dark eyes glistening with tears. She looked horrified. Utterly. Completely. The light was gone. His light.

"Yes," he said, his voice rough. "Can you guess what he did?"

"What?" The word was scarcely a whisper.

"He laughed. And he said, 'Just as I thought, you are my son.' He told me that no matter how I dressed it up, no matter how I pretended I had morals, I was just as blood-thirsty as he was. Just as hungry for vengeance and to have what I thought should be mine, in the fashion I saw fit. And then he walked back into the warehouse."

"What did you do?"

Matteo remembered the moment vividly. Remembered waiting for a minute, watching, letting his father's words sink in. Recognizing the truth of them. And embracing them fully. He was his father's son. And if he, or anyone else, stood a chance of ever breaking free, it had to end.

The front end of the warehouse had collapsed and Matteo had stood back, looking on, his hand curled around his phone. He could have called emergency services. He could have tried to save Benito.

But he hadn't. Instead, he'd turned his back, the heat blistering behind him, a spark falling onto his neck, singeing his flesh. And then he'd walked away. And he hadn't looked back, not once. And in that moment he was the full embodiment of everything his father had trained him to be.

He'd found out about Carlo's and Benito's deaths over the phone the next day. And there had been no more denial, no more hiding. No more believing that somewhere deep down he was good. That he had a hope of redemption.

He had let it burn in the warehouse.

"I let him die," he said. "I watched him go in, watched as the front end of the building collapsed. I could have called someone, and I didn't. I made the choice to be the man he always wanted me to be. The man I always was. I turned and I walked away. I did just as I promised I would do. I let him burn, with all of his damned money. And I can't regret the choice. He made his, I made mine. And everyone is free of him now. Of both of them."

Alessia was waxen, her skin pale, her lips tinged blue. "I don't know what to say."

"Do you see, Alessia? This is what I was trying to tell you. What you need to understand." He leaned forward, extending his hand to her, and she jerked back. Her withdrawal felt like a stab to the chest, but it was no less than he deserved. "I'm not the hero of the story. I am nothing less than the villain."

She understood now, he could see it, along with a dawning horror in her eyes that he wanted to turn away from. She was afraid. Afraid of him. He wasn't her knight anymore.

"I think maybe I should wait a few days to have my things moved into your room," she said after a long moment of silence.

He nodded. "That might be wise." Pain assaulted him and he tried to ignore it, tried to grit his teeth and sit with a neutral expression.

"I'll talk to you later?"

"Of course." He sat back on the couch and watched her leave. Then he closed his eyes and tried to picture her smile again. Tried to recapture the way she'd looked at him just a few moments before. But instead of her light, all he could see was a haunted expression, one he had put there.

* * *

Alessia was gasping for breath by the time she got to her bedroom. She closed the door behind her and put her hand on her chest, felt her heart hammering beneath her palm.

Matteo had let Benito and Carlo die.

She sucked in a shuddering breath and started pacing back and forth, fighting the tears that were threatening to spill down her cheeks.

She replayed what he had said again in her mind. He hadn't forced Benito or Carlo back into the burning building. Hadn't caused them harm with his own hands.

He had walked away. He had washed his hands and walked away, accepting in that moment whatever the consequences might be.

Alessia walked over to her bed and sat on the edge of it. And she tried to reconcile the man downstairs with the man she'd always believed him to be.

The man beneath the armor wasn't perfect. He was wounded, damaged beyond reason. Hurting. And for the first time she really understood what that meant. Understood how shut down he was. How much it would take to reach him.

And she wasn't sure if she could do it. Wasn't sure she had the strength to do it.

It had been so much easier when he was simply the fantasy. When he was the man she'd made him be in her mind. When he was an ideal, a man sent to ride to her rescue.

She'd put him in that position. From the moment she'd first seen him. Then after he had rescued her, she'd assigned him that place even more so.

The night of her bachelorette party…

"Damn you, Alessia," she said to herself.

Because she'd done it then, too. She'd used Matteo as part of her fantasy, as part of the little world she'd built up in her mind to keep herself from crumbling. She had taken him on her own terms, used him to fill a void, and never once had she truly looked into his. Never once had she truly tried to fill it.

Being there for Matteo, knowing him, meant knowing this. Meant knowing that he had faced down a terrible decision, and that he had made a terrible choice.

The wrong choice, at least in traditional terms of right and wrong.

Very few people would hold it against him that he hadn't raced into the burning building after his father, but to know that he had also not called for help. That he had meant what he'd said to his father. That he would let him, and all of it, burn. In flame. In greed. And he had.

Her lover, her Matteo, had a core of ice and steel. Getting through it, finding his heart, might be impossible. She faced that, truly faced it, for the first time.

Matteo might never love. The ending might not really be happy. The truth was, she lived her life in denial. The pursuit of contentment at least, at all costs, and if that required denial, then she employed it, and she'd always done it quite effectively.

Walking down the aisle toward Alessandro had been the first time she'd truly realized that if she didn't do something, if she didn't stop it, it wouldn't stop itself.

She wrapped her arms around herself, cold driving through her. She had another choice to make. A choice about Matteo. And she wouldn't make it lightly.

There was no sugarcoating this. No putting on blinders. It was what the wives of these Corretti men, of the Battaglia men, had always done. Looked the other way while their husbands sank into destruction and depravity, but she wouldn't do that.

If she was going to be Matteo's wife, in every sense, then she would face it all head-on.

It was empty to make a commitment to someone if

you were pretending they were someone they weren't. It was empty to say you loved someone if you only loved a mirage.

Love. She had been afraid of that word in connection to Matteo for so long, and yet, she knew that was what it was. What it had always been. At least, she'd loved what she'd known about him.

Now she knew more. Now she was going to have to figure out whether she loved the idea, or the man.

Matteo lay in bed. It was past midnight. Hours since he'd last seen Alessia. Hours since they'd spoken.

His body ached, a bleeding wound in his chest where his heart should be. The absence of the heart was nothing new, but the pain was. He had lived in numbness for so long, and Alessia had come back into his life.

Then things had started to change. He'd started to want again. Started to feel again. And now he felt like he was torn open, like the healed, scarred-over, nerveless pieces of himself had been scrubbed raw again. Like he was starting over, starting back at the boy he'd been. The one who had been taken into his father's hands and molded, hard and cruel, into the image the older man had wanted to see.

He felt weak. Vulnerable in a way he could never recall feeling at any point in his life.

Alessia had walked away from him, and he couldn't blame her. In a way, it comforted him. Because at least she hadn't simply blithely walked on in her illusion of who she wanted him to be. She had heard his words. And she'd believed them.

He should be completely grateful for that. Should be happy that she knew. That she wasn't committed to a man who didn't truly exist.

But he couldn't be happy. Selfishly, he wanted her back.

Wanted the light and heat and smiles. Wanted one person to look at him and see hope.

"Matteo?"

He looked up and saw Alessia standing in the doorway, her dark hair loose around her shoulders.

"Yes?" He pushed into a sitting position.

"I felt like I owed it to you to really think about what you said."

"And you owed it to you."

She nodded. "I suppose I did."

"And what conclusion have you come to?"

"You aren't the man I thought you were."

The words hit him with the force of a moving truck. "No. I'm sure in all of your fantasies about me you never once dreamed that I was a killer."

She shook her head. "I didn't. I still don't think you're that. I don't think you're perfect, either, but I don't think it was ever terribly fair of me to try to make you perfect. You had your own life apart from me. Your own experiences. My mistake was believing that everything began and ended during the times our eyes met over the garden wall. In my mind, when you held me after the attack, you went somewhere hazy, somewhere I couldn't picture. I didn't think about what you did after, not really. I didn't think of the reality of you returning home, covered in blood. I didn't think about what your father might have said to you. I knew Benito Corretti was a bad man, but for some reason I never imagined how it might have touched you. I only ever pictured you in the context of my world, my dreams and where you fit into them. It was my mistake, not yours."

"But I wouldn't have blamed you if you never imagined that. No one did. Not even my family, I'm certain of that."

"Still, I wasn't looking at you like you were a real person. And you were right to make me see."

"Alessia, if you want—"

"Let me finish. I see now. I see you, Matteo, not just the fantasy I created. And I don't want to walk away. I want to stay with you. I want to make a family with you."

"You trust me to help raise your child after you found out what I'm capable of?"

"That night of your life can't live in isolation. It's connected to the rest of your life, to all of it. To who your father was, the history of what he'd done to other people, to what he'd done to you."

"He never did anything to me, he just—"

"He forced you to do things you would never have done. He made you violate your conscience, over and over again until it was scarred. He would have turned you into a monster."

"He did, Alessia. That's the point. He did."

She shook her head. "You put a stop to it."

"I had to," he said, his voice rough. "I had to because you don't just walk away from the Correttis. It's not possible. My father would not have released his hold."

"I know. I understand."

"And you absolve me?"

"You don't need my absolution."

"But do I have it?" he asked, desperate for it, craving it more than his next breath.

She nodded. "If I have yours."

"For what?"

"For what I did. For not telling you about Alessandro. For agreeing to marry him in the first place. For trapping you in this marriage."

"You didn't trap me."

"You said—"

"Alessia, I have been manipulated into doing things far worse than marrying you, and I have done it with much greater coercion. A little news piece on what a jerk I am for not making your child legitimate was hardly going to force my hand."

"Then why did you do it?"

"To cement the deal. To give our child my name. All things I could have walked away from."

"Then forgive me, at least, for lying to you. For leaving you in the hotel room."

"I do. I was angry about it, but only because it felt so wrong to watch you walking toward him. To know that he would have you and not me. If I had known that there was a deal on the table that could be secured by marriage to you I would have been the one volunteering for the job."

A ghost of a smile touched her lips. "When my father first told me about the deal with the Correttis, that it would be sealed by marriage, I said yes immediately. I was so sure it would be you. And when it was Alessandro who showed up at the door to talk terms the next day I thought…I thought I would die."

"Waiting for your knight to rescue you?"

"Yes. I was. But I've stopped doing that now. I need to learn to rescue myself. To make my own decisions."

"You've certainly been doing that over the past couple of months."

"I have. And some of them have been bad, ill-timed decisions, but they've been mine. And I want you to know that I've made another decision."

"What is that?"

"You're my husband. And I'll take you as you are. Knowing your past, knowing the kind of man you can be. I want you to understand that I'm not sugarcoating it, or glossing over the truth. I understand what you did. I understand that…that you don't feel emotion the same way that I do. The same way most people do."

"Do you really understand that? I keep it on a leash for

a reason, Alessia, a very important reason, and I won't compromise it."

She nodded. "I know."

"And still you want to try? You want to be my wife? To let me have a hand in raising our child?"

"Yes. No matter what, you're the father of my child, Matteo, and there is no revelation that can change that. I don't want to change that."

"How can you say that with such confidence?"

"Because no matter what you might have done, you aren't cruel."

She leaned in and he took a strand of her hair between his thumb and forefinger. Soft like silk. He wanted to feel it brushing over his skin. Wanted to drown out this moment, drown out his pain, with physical pleasure.

"Am I not?" he asked.

"No."

"You're wrong there," he said. "So very wrong. I am selfish, a man who thinks of his own pleasure, his own comfort, above all else. No matter how I pretend otherwise."

"That isn't true."

"Yes, it is. Even now, all I can think about is what your bare skin will feel like beneath my hands. All I want is to lose myself in you."

"Then do it."

His every muscle locked up, so tight it was painful. "Alessia, don't."

"What?"

"Don't sacrifice yourself for me!" he roared. "Don't do this because you feel sorry for me."

"I'm not." She took a step toward him. "I want this because I want to be close to you. To know you. To be your wife in every way." A smile tugged at the corners of her lips. "I'm also not opposed to the orgasms you're so good at giving me. This is by no means unselfish on my part, trust me."

His skin felt like it was burning. Or perhaps that was the blood beneath his skin. Either way, he felt like he would be consumed by his need. His desire. Passion he swore he would never allow himself to feel.

Emotion he swore he would never feel.

But in this moment with Alessia, her eyes so bright and intense, so honest, he could hold back nothing. Deny her nothing. Least of all this.

She knew the truth, and still she wanted him. Not as a perfect figure, a knight in shining armor, but as the man he was. It was a gift he didn't deserve, a gift he should turn away, because he had no right to it.

But he had spoken the truth. He was selfish. Far too selfish to do anything but take what was on offer.

"Show me you want me." His words were rough, forced through his tightened throat. "Show me you still want me." Those words echoed through his soul, tearing through him, leaving him raw and bleeding inside.

Alessia wrapped one arm around his neck, her fingers laced in his hair, and put the other on his cheek. She pressed a kiss to his lips, soft, gentle. Purposeful. "Always."

There was no hope of him being noble, not now, not tonight. But then, that shouldn't be a surprise. He didn't do noble. He didn't do selfless. And it wouldn't start now.

He kissed her, deep and hard, his body throbbing, his heart raging. He wrapped his arms around her and pulled her in close, reveling in the feel of her. Touching Alessia was a thrill that he didn't think would ever become commonplace. He had hungered for her touch, for her closeness, for so many years, and he knew his desire for it would never fade.

If anything, it only grew.

He slid his hands down her waist, over her hips, her thighs, and gripped her hard, tugging her up into his arms, those long, lean legs wrapping around his waist as he walked them both to the bed.

Alessia started working on the knot on his tie, her movements shaky and clumsy and all the sexier for it. He sat on the bed, and Alessia remained on top of him, now resting on her knees. She tugged hard on the tie and managed to get it off, then started working at the buttons on his shirt.

He continued to kiss her, deep and desperate, pushing her dress up, past her hips, her waist, her breasts, and over her head. Her lips were swollen from kissing, her face flushed, her hair disheveled from where he'd run his fingers through it.

She looked wild, free, the most beautiful thing he'd ever seen. But then, Alessia had been, from the moment he'd seen her, the most beautiful sight he'd ever beheld. And then, when his vision of her had been one of innocence, protectiveness, it had been all about that glow that was inside of her.

He could see it, along with the outer beauty that drove him to madness. Now that their lives, their feelings, had no more innocence left, he could still see it. Still feel it deep inside of him, an ache that wouldn't ease.

She pushed his shirt off his shoulders, the buttoned cuffs snagging on his hands. A little growl escaped her lips. He wrapped one hand around her waist to hold her steady and lay back on the bed, leaving her perched over him, then he undid the buttons as quickly as possible and tossed the shirt to the side.

Alessia moved away from him, standing in front of the bed, in front of him. She met his eyes, and put her hands behind her back, her movement quick. Her bra loosened, then fell, baring her breasts to him. His stomach tightened, he could barely breathe.

She smiled, then hooked her fingers into the sides of her panties and tugged them off.

He wanted to say something. To tell her how beautiful she was, how perfect. But he couldn't speak. He could only watch, held completely under her spell.

She approached the bed, her fingers deft on his belt buckle, making quick work of his pants and underwear, and leaving him as naked as she was.

"You're so much more…just so much more than I ever imagined," she said. "I made fantasies about you, but they were a girl's fantasies. I'm not a girl, though, I'm a woman. And I'm glad you're not only that one-dimensional imagining I had of you. I'm glad you're you."

She leaned in, running the tip of her finger along the length of his rock-hard erection. Every thought ran from his head like water, his heart thundering in his ears.

Lush lips curved into a wicked smile and she leaned in, flicking her tongue over the head of his shaft. "I've never done this before. So you have to tell me if I do it wrong."

"You couldn't possibly do it wrong," he said, not sure how he managed to speak at all. It shouldn't be possible when he couldn't breathe.

And she proved him right. Her mouth on him hot, sweet torture that streaked through his veins like flame. But where other flames destroyed, this fire cleansed. He sifted his fingers through her hair, needing an anchor. Needing to touch her, to be a part of this. Not simply on the receiving end of the pleasure she was giving him.

He needed more. Needed to taste her, too.

"Get on the bed," he growled.

She complied, not abandoning her task as she got up onto the bed, onto her knees. He sat up and she raised her head, her expression confused. Then he grasped her hips and maneuvered her around so that she was over him, so that he could taste her like she was tasting him.

She gasped when his tongue touched her.

"Don't stop," he said, the command rough, firmer than he'd intended it to be, but she didn't seem to mind.

He slipped a finger inside of her while he pleasured her with his tongue, and she gasped again, freezing for a moment before taking him fully into her mouth. His head fell back, a harsh groan on his lips.

"I can't last much longer," he said.

"Neither can I," she panted, moving away from him, returning a moment later, her thighs on either side of his. She bent down and pressed a kiss to his lips. "Ready?" she asked.

"More than."

She positioned her body so that the head of his erection met with her slick entrance, then she lowered herself down onto him, so slowly he thought he would be consumed utterly by the white heat moving through him.

She moved over him, her eyes locked with his. He grasped her hips, meeting each of her thrusts, watching her face, watching her pleasure.

He moved his hand, pressed his palm flat over her stomach, then slid it upward to cup one of her breasts. He liked the view. Liked being able to see all of her as she brought them both to the brink.

She leaned forward, kissing his lips, her breath getting harsher, faster, her movements more erratic. He lowered his hand back to her hip and strengthened his own movements, pushing them farther, faster.

They both reached the edge at the same time, and when he tipped over into the abyss, all he could do was hold on to her as release rushed through him like a wave, leaving no part of him untouched. No part of him hidden.

When the storm passed, Alessia was with him.

She rested her head on his chest, her breath hot on

his skin. He wrapped his arms tight around her, held her to him.

He would keep her with him, no matter what.

Yes, he was a selfish bastard.

But in this moment, he couldn't regret it. If it meant keeping Alessia, he never would.

CHAPTER TWELVE

ALESSIA WOKE UP a few hours later, feeling cold. She wasn't sure why. It was a warm evening, and she had blankets, and Matteo, to keep her warm.

Matteo.

He made her heart feel like it was cracking apart. She wanted to reach him. Wanted to touch him. Really touch him, not just with her hands on his skin, but to touch his heart.

This was so close to what she wanted. A baby. The man she loved. *Dio*, she loved him so much. It made her hurt. Not just for her, but for him. For what she knew they could have that he seemed determined to wall himself off from.

A tear slipped down her cheek and she sat up, getting out of bed and crossing to the window. Now she was crying. She wasn't really sure why she was crying, either.

But she was. Really crying. From somewhere deep inside of herself. From a bottomless well that seemed to have opened up in her.

Why did she never get what she wanted? Why was it always out of reach?

Her mother's love had been there, so briefly, long enough for her to have tasted it, to know what it was. Just so she could feel the ache keenly when it was gone? And then there was Matteo. The man she'd wanted all her life. Her hero. Her heart's desire.

And when her father said she would marry a Corretti, of course it was Matteo who had come to mind. But she'd been given to Alessandro instead. And then, one more chance, Matteo at the hotel. And she'd managed to mess that up.

In the end, she'd gotten Matteo, but in the clumsiest, most dishonest way imaginable. Not telling him she was engaged, announcing to the world she was pregnant, forcing him to marry her, in a sense.

And now there was this…this heat between them that didn't go deeper than skin on his side. This love that was burning a hole through her soul, that he would never, ever be able to return.

"Alessia?" She turned and saw Matteo sitting up, his voice filled with concern. "Are you okay? Did I hurt you?"

"No." She shook her head. And he hadn't. She'd hurt herself. "I was just…thinking." There was no point in hiding the tears. Her voice was wobbly, watery. Too late to bother with the fiction that she was fine.

"About what?"

She bit her lip. Then opted for some form of honesty. "I've been pretending."

"What do you mean?"

"My whole life. I thought if I pretended to be happy, if I made the best of what I had, that I would be okay not having it all. That if I smiled enough I would get past my mother being gone. That my father's most recent slap to my face hadn't hurt me deeper than I wanted to admit. I had to, because someone had to show my brothers and sisters that you made a choice about how you handled life. We only had what we had, and I didn't want them…I didn't want them to be sad, or to see me sad. So I protected them from what I could. I made sure they didn't know how hard it was. How bad it was. I've been carrying around the burden of everyone's happiness and just trying to make what

I had work. But I'm not happy." It burst from her, truer than any words she'd ever spoken. "I don't want to smile about my childhood. It was horrible. My father was horrible. And I had to care for my siblings and it was so hard." She wiped at a tear on her cheek, tried to stop her hands from shaking. But she couldn't.

She couldn't stop shaking.

"I love them, so much, so I hate to even admit this but...I was willing to give everything for them. And no one...no one has ever given even the smallest thing for me. And I'm sorry if that makes me a bad person but I want someone to care. I want someone to care about me."

"Alessia..."

"I'm sorry," she said, wiping at more tears. "This is... probably hormones talking."

"Is it?"

She nodded, biting her lip to keep a sob from escaping. "I'm feeling sorry for myself a little too late."

"Tell me what you want, Alessia."

It was a command, and since he was the first person to ever ask, she felt compelled to answer.

"I wish someone loved me."

"Your brothers and sisters do."

She nodded. "I know they do."

Matteo watched Alessia, her body bent in despair, her expression desolate, and felt like someone was stabbing him.

Her admission was so stark, so painful. He realized then that he had put her in a position, as his angel, his light, and he had never once sought out whether or not she needed something.

He was taking from her instead. Draining her light. Using it to illuminate the dark and void places in himself. Using her to warm his soul, and he was costing her.

Just another person intent on taking from her for his own selfish needs.

"It's not the same as what you mean, though, is it?" he asked slowly.

"It's just...I can't really be myself around them," she said. "I can't show them my pain. I can't...I can't let my guard drop for a moment because then they might know, and they'll feel like they're a burden, and I just...don't want them to carry that. It's not fair."

"But what about you?"

"What about me?"

Matteo felt like someone had placed a rock in his stomach. Only hours ago, he had been content to hold Alessia tight against him. Content to keep her because she had accepted who he was, hadn't she?

But he saw now. He saw that Alessia accepted far less than she should. That she gave at the expense of herself. That she would keep doing it until the light in her had been used up. And he would be the worst offender. Because he was too closed off, too dark, to offer anything in return.

Sex wouldn't substitute, no matter how much he wanted to pretend it might. That as long as he could keep her sleepy, and naked and satisfied, he was giving.

But they were having a baby, a child. She was his wife. And life, the need for support, for touch, for caring, went well outside the bedroom. He knew that, as keenly as he knew he couldn't give it.

"I have to go," he said, his words leaden.

"What?"

"I have to go down to my offices for a few hours."

"It's four in the morning."

"I know, but this cannot wait."

"Okay," she said.

Damn her for accepting it. Damn him for making her. He bent down and started collecting his clothes, running his fingers over his silk tie, remembering how she'd undone it only hours before with shaking fingers. How she'd kissed him. How she'd given to him.

He dressed quickly, Alessia still standing by the window, frozen, watching him.

He did the buttons on his shirt cuffs and opened his closet, retrieving his suit jacket. Then he took a breath, and turned his back on Alessia.

"I should be back later today. Feel free to go back to bed."

"In here?"

"Perhaps it would be best if you went back to your room. You haven't had your things moved, after all."

"But I made my decision."

"Perhaps I haven't made mine."

"You said you had earlier."

"Yes, I did, and then you decided you needed more time to think about it. Now I would like an extension, as well. That seems fair, doesn't it?"

He took his phone off the nightstand and curled his fingers around it. A flashback assaulted him. Of how it had been when he'd turned his back on the burning warehouse, leaving the people inside of it to deal with the consequences of their actions without his help.

But this was different. He was walking away for different reasons. It wasn't about freeing himself. This was about freeing her.

And when he returned home later in the day, perhaps he would have the strength to do it. To do what needed to be done.

Alessia didn't go back to sleep. Instead, she wandered around the palazzo like a zombie, trying to figure out why she'd exploded all over Matteo like that. And why he'd responded like he had.

It was this love business. It sucked, in her opinion.

Suddenly she'd felt like she was being torn open, like she was too full to hold everything in. Like she'd glossed over everything with that layer of contentment she'd become so good at cultivating.

She wanted more than that, and she wasn't sure why. Wasn't sure why she couldn't just keep making the best of things. She had Matteo. That should be enough.

But it wasn't.

Because you don't really have him.

She didn't. She had his name. She was married to him. She was having his baby, sharing his bed and his body, but she didn't really have him. Because the core of him remained off-limits to her. Not just her, but to everyone.

She wanted it all. Whether she should or not. Whether it made sense or not. But that was love. Which brought her back around to love sucking. Because if she could just put on a smile and deal with it, if she could just take what he was giving and not ask for any more, she was sure there could be some kind of happiness there.

But there wouldn't be joy. There wouldn't be anything deep and lasting. And she was tired of taking less than what she wanted to keep from making waves. She was so tired of it she thought she might break beneath the strain of it.

"Buongiorno."

Alessia turned and saw Matteo standing in the doorway, his hair a mess, as though he'd run his fingers through it a few too many times, his tie undone, his shirt unbuttoned at the collar. His jacket had been discarded somewhere else.

"Hello, Matteo. Did you have a good day at work?"

"I didn't go to work," he said.

His admission hit her hard. "You didn't?"

"No. I was running again. Like I did the day of your first wedding. That was what I did, you know. You asked me to go to the airport, and I nearly went. But in the end I was too angry at you. For lying. For being ready to marry him. So I went to my house in Germany, mainly because no one knows about it. And I did my best to be impossible to reach, because I didn't want to deal with any accusations. I didn't want to hear from my family. And I didn't want to hear from you, because I knew you would be too much of a temptation for me to resist. That if I read your emails or listened to your messages, I would want you back. That I would come back to you."

"So you hid instead?"

"It was easier. And today I thought I might do the same thing. Because I don't like to see you cry. I don't like seeing you sad, knowing that it's my fault."

"It's not your fault."

"Mainly I just drove," he said, as if she hadn't spoken. "A little too fast, but that's what a Ferrari is for."

"I suppose so."

"I've come to a decision."

"Wait, before you say anything, I want to say something."

"Why is it your turn?"

"Because you left this morning before I could finish. All right, not really, I didn't know what I was going to say then. But I do now."

"And what are you going to say?"

"I love you, Matteo. I think, in some ways, I always have. But more over the past months, more still when you told me your story. I am in love with you, and I want you to love me back. I'm tired of not having everything, and I think you and I could have everything. But you have to let us."

"Alessia…I can't."

"You can, you just have to….you have to…"

"What? I have to forget a lifetime of conditioning? I

have to ignore the fact that my losing control, that my embracing emotion, might have horrible, devastating consequences, not just for you, but for our child? I have to ignore what I know to be true about myself, about my blood, and just...let it all go? Do you want me to just forget that I'm the sort of man who walked away and left his father to die in a burning warehouse? To just take that off like old clothes and put on something new? It wouldn't work. Even if it did it would be dangerous. I can't forget. I have to keep control."

"I don't believe you," she said.

"You don't believe me? Did you not listen to what I told you? Did you not understand? All of that, breaking that man's legs, leaving my father, that was what I am capable of when I have the most rigid control of myself. What I did to those men who attacked you? That blind rage? I didn't know what I was doing. I had no control, and if you hadn't stopped me...I would have killed them. I would have killed them and never felt an ounce of guilt for it."

"So you would have killed rapists, am I supposed to believe that makes you a bad, horrible, irredeemable person? That you would have done what you had to do to save a young girl?"

"That isn't the point," he said. "As long as I control it...as long as I don't feel, I won't do something I regret. I won't do something beyond myself. Even with control, do you see what I can do? What I have done? I can never afford to let it go. I can't afford—"

"I don't believe it. That isn't it. You're running scared, Matteo. You aren't afraid of losing control, you're afraid that if you feel you're going to have to face the guilt. The grief. You're hiding from the consequences of your actions. Hiding behind this blessed wall of cold and ice, but you can't live there forever."

"Yes, I can."

"No, you can't. Because at least for the sake of our child, our baby, Matteo, you have to break out of it."

"Has it ever once occurred to you that I don't want to?" he roared. "I don't want to feel, Alessia, I damn well don't. I don't want to face what I've done. To feel the full impact of my life. Of what was done to me. I don't want it. I don't need it. And I don't want you."

She stepped back, her body going numb suddenly. Shock. It must be that. Her body's defense because if it allowed her to feel the pain, she would collapse at his feet.

"You don't want me?" she asked.

"No. I never did. Not outside the bedroom. I told you that if you didn't expect love we would be fine. It was the one thing I told you could never be. I said no love. I promised faithfulness, a place in my home, my bed, what more did you want? I offered everything!"

"You offered me nothing," she said, her voice quivering, a slow ache starting to break through the numbness, shards of pain pushing through. "None of that means anything if you're withholding the only thing I really want."

"My love is so important? When has love ever given you anything but pain, Alessia?"

"I don't know because I've never had it for long enough to see."

"Then why make it so important?"

"Because I deserve it!" She broke then, tears spilling down her cheeks. "Don't I deserve it, Matteo?"

Matteo's face paled, and he took a step back. "Yes."

She didn't take it as a sign that she had gotten what she wanted. No, Matteo looked like someone had died.

She didn't say anything. She just waited.

"You deserve that," he said finally. "And you won't get it from me."

"Can't you just try?"

He shook his head. "I can't."

"Stop being so bloody noble. Stop being so repressed. Fight for us. Fight for this."

"No. I won't hold you to me. I won't hold you to this. That is one thing I will do for you, one thing I'll do right."

"You really think removing yourself is the only way to fix something? Keeping yourself distant?" It broke her heart. More than his rejection, it was his view of himself that left her crippled with pain.

"It's a kindness, Alessia. The best thing I've ever done. Trust me."

He turned and walked out of the room, left her standing there in the massive sitting area by herself. She couldn't cry. Couldn't bring herself to make the sound of pain that was building inside her. Endless. Bereft.

She wanted to collapse. But she couldn't. Because she had to stand strong for her child. Matteo might have walked away, but it didn't change the fact that they were having a baby. Didn't change the fact that she would be a mother in under six months.

It didn't change the fact that, no matter what, she loved Matteo Corretti with everything she had in her.

But she would never go back and demand less. Would never undo what she'd said to him. Because she had a right to ask for more. Had a right to expect more. She was willing to give to Matteo. To love him no matter who he was. No matter what he had done.

But she needed his love in return. Because she wasn't playing at love, it was real. And she refused to play at happiness, to feign joy.

She sank into one of the plush love seats, the pain from her chest spreading to the rest of her body.

She had a feeling there would be no happiness, fake or genuine, for a very long time.

CHAPTER THIRTEEN

MATTEO DIDN'T BOTHER with alcohol this time. He didn't deserve to have any of the reality of the past few hours blunted for his own comfort. He deserved for it to cut him open.

He shifted into Fifth and pushed harder on the gas pedal. Driving always helped him sort through things. And it helped him get farther away from his problems while he did it. But Alessia didn't feel any farther away.

She was with him. In him. Beneath his skin and, he feared, past his defenses.

Those defenses he had just given all to protect.

You aren't afraid of losing control, you're afraid that if you feel you're going to have to face the guilt.

That was just what he was. Afraid. To his very core.

He was scared that if he reached a hand out and asked for redemption it would truly be beyond his reach. He was afraid that if he let the door open on his emotions there would be nothing but pain, and grief, and the unending lash of guilt for all he had done, both under his father's influence, and the night of the fire.

He was afraid that he would expose himself, let himself feel it all, and he would still fall short for Alessia. That he wouldn't know how to be a real husband, or a real father.

He was afraid to want it. Afraid to try it.

She wanted him to fight for them. Nothing good came from him fighting.

Except the time you saved her.

Yes, there was that. He had always held that moment up as a banner displaying what happened when he lost control. A reminder that, as dangerous as he was in general, it was when he felt passion that he truly became a monster.

He pulled his car over to the side of the road, heart pounding, and he closed his eyes, let himself picture that day fully.

The fear in Alessia's eyes. The way those men had touched her. The rage that had poured through him.

And he knew one thing for certain in that moment. That no matter how blinded he was by anger, he would never hurt Alessia. He would never hurt his child. No, his emotions, not his mind, told him emphatically that he would die before he let any harm come to them.

That he would give everything to keep them safe.

He had been so certain, all this time, that his mind would protect him, but it had been his heart that had demanded he do whatever it took to save Alessia Battaglia from harm. It had been his heart that had demanded he spend that night in New York with her.

And it was his heart that was crumbling into pieces now. There was no protecting his defenses, because Alessia had slipped in beneath them years ago, before they had fully formed, and she was destroying them now from the inside out.

Matteo put his head on the steering wheel, his body shaking as pain worked its way through him, spreading through his veins like poison.

Something in him cracked open, every feeling, every desire, every deep need, suddenly acute and sharp. It was too much. Because it was everything all at once. Grief for the boy he'd been, for the man his father had become and what the end had done to both of them. Justification because he'd done what he had for his whole family. To free everyone. To free himself. Guilt, anguish, because in some ways he would always regret it.

And a desperate longing for redemption. A desperate wish he could go back to the beginning, to the start of it all, and take the path that would form him into Alessia's white knight. So that he could truly be the man she'd seen.

Alessia. He thought of her face. Her bright smile. Her tears.

Of meeting her eyes in the mirror at a bar, and feeling a sense of certainty, so deep, so true, he hadn't even tried to fight it.

And he felt something else. A light, flooding through his soul, touching everything. Only this time, it wasn't brief. Wasn't temporary. It stayed. It shone on everything, the ugly, the unfinished and the good. It showed him for what he was, what he could be.

Love. He loved Alessia. He had loved her all of his life.

And he wasn't the man that she should have. He wasn't the man he could have been if things had gone differently.

But with love came hope. A hope that he could try. A hope for redemption. A hope for the future.

For every dirty, broken feeling that he'd unleashed inside of him, he had let loose the good to combat it.

He had never imagined that. Had never believed that there was so much lightness in him.

It was Alessia. His love for her. His hope for their future.

He might not be the man she'd once imagined. He might not be the man he might have been in different circumstances. But that man was the one that Alessia deserved and no less.

So he would become that man. Because he loved Alessia too much to offer her less.

Matteo picked up his phone, and dialed a number he rarely used if he could help it. But this was the start. The start of changing. He was too tired to keep fighting, anyway. Too tired to continue a rivalry he simply didn't want to be involved in. A rivalry created by his father, by Alessandro's father. They both hated those bastards so what was the point of honoring a hatred created and fostered by them?

No more. It had to end.

"Corretti."

"It's Matteo."

"Ah, Matteo." Alessandro didn't sound totally thrilled to hear from him.

"How is everything going? In terms of unifying the business?"

"Fine."

"Great. That's not exactly why I called."

"Why did you call, then? I'm a little busy."

"I called because I want to make sure that as we unify the company, we unify the family, as well. I…I don't want to keep any of this rivalry alive. I've been holding on to some things for far too long that I need to let go. This is one of them."

"Accepting my superiority?"

"If that's what it takes."

Alessandro paused for a moment. "You aren't dying, are you?"

"It feels like it. But I think it will pass." It had to. "I don't want to carry things on like Carlo and Benito did, and I don't just mean the criminal activity. If we have a problem, I say we just punch each other in the face and get it over with, rather than creating a multigenerational feud."

"That works for me."

"Good. See you at the next meeting." He hung up. It wasn't like he needed to hug it out with his cousin or anything, but he was ready to start putting things behind him. To stop shielding himself from the past and embrace the future.

A future that would include Alessia.

Alessia looked up when the Ferrari roared back onto the grounds. She was standing in the garden, doing her best to at least enjoy the waning sunlight. It was better than the whole dissolving-into-never-ending-tears bit.

Matteo left the car in the middle of the drive and strode into the yard, his eyes fixed on hers. When he reached her, he pulled her into his arms, his expression fierce. Then he lowered his head and kissed her. Long. Deep. Intense.

She wrapped her arms around his neck and kissed him back, her face wet, tasting salt from tears. She didn't know whose. She didn't care.

She didn't want to ask questions now, she just wanted to live in this moment. When they parted, Matteo buried his face in her neck and held her tight. And she held him, too. Neither of them moved, neither of them spoke.

Emotion swelled in her chest, so big she wasn't sure she could stand it. Wasn't sure she could breathe around it.

"I love you," he said. "I have never said it before, Alessia. Not to anyone. Not to a woman, not to family. So when I say it, I mean it. With everything I have, such as it is. I love you."

A sob broke through her lips and she tightened her hold on him. "I love you, too."

"Still?"

"Always."

"You were right. I was afraid. I'm still afraid. But I can't hide anymore. You made it impossible. I want to be the man worthy of that look you used to give me. I want to be everything for you, I don't just want to take from you. I was content to just take that light you carry around in you, Alessia. To let it warm me. But you deserve more than that. So I'll be more than that. I'm not everything I should be. I'm broken. I've done things that were wrong. I've seen things no man should have to see. But I will give you everything that I have to give, and then I'll reach deep and find more, because you're right, you deserve it all. And I want you, so that means I have to figure out a way to be it all."

"Matteo, no, you don't. You just have to meet me in the middle. And love will cover our shortcomings."

"Just meet you in the middle?"

"Mainly, I just need you to love me."

"That I can do, Alessia Corretti. I've been doing it for most of my life."

"You might not believe this, Matteo, but as you are, you're my knight in shining armor. You are flawed. You've been through unimaginable things, and you love anyway. You're so strong, so brave, so utterly perfect. Well, not perfect, but perfect for me. You're the only man I've ever wanted, the only man I've ever loved. And that will never change."

"How is it that you see me, all of me, and love me, anyway?"

"That's what love is. And you know what? It's not hard to love you. You're brave, honorable. You were willing to cut off any chance at having your own happiness to try to protect the people around you. To try to do right. You're the most incredible man I've ever known."

"Quite the compliment coming from the most amazing woman. Your bravery, your willingness to love, in spite of all you've been through, that's what pulled me out of the darkness. Your light won. Your love won."

"I'm so glad it did."

He put his hand on Alessia's stomach. "This is what I want. You, me, our baby. I was too afraid before to admit how much I wanted it. Too afraid I didn't deserve it, that I would lose it. I'm still afraid I don't deserve it, but I want it so much." He leaned in and kissed her lips. "I'm not cold anymore."

"Never again," she said.

He wrapped his arms tight around her and spun them both in a circle. She laughed, and so did he. Genuine. Happy. Joy bloomed inside of her. Joy like she'd never felt before. Real, true. And for her. Not to keep those around her smiling.

"We agreed on one night. This is turning into a lot longer than one night," he said when they stopped spinning.

"It is," she said. "All things considered, I was thinking we might want to make it forever."

"Forever sounds about right."

EPILOGUE

THE CORRETTIS WERE all together. But unlike at the funerals that had been the most common reason for them to come together in the past, unlike Alessia and Alessandro's wedding-that-wasn't, there was no veiled animosity here at the celebration of Teresa's birthday. And not just Teresa's birthday, but the regeneration of the docklands. The culmination of a joint family effort. Of them coming together.

After the big ceremony down at the docklands, they'd returned to the family estate.

They had all sat down to dinner together. They had all talked, business and personal, and not a single punch had been thrown. And it wasn't only Correttis. Some of the Battaglias, Alessia's siblings, were there, as well.

Matteo considered it a resounding success.

After dinner, they all sat in the garden, lights strung overhead, a warm breeze filtering through. And Matteo felt peace.

"Hey there." Alessia walked away from where she'd been talking to his sister Lia and came to stand beside him, their daughter, Luciana Battaglia-Corretti, on her hip.

"The most beautiful women here have graced me with their presence. I am content," he said, brushing his knuckles over Alessia's cheek and dropping a kiss onto Luciana's soft head.

Matteo looked at his wife and daughter, at his family,

all of them, surrounding him. That word meant something new now. The Correttis were no longer at war.

He bent down and extracted Luciana from her mother's arms, pulling his daughter close, the warm weight of her, her absolute trust in him, something he would never take for granted.

Alessia smiled at him, her eyes shining, her face glowing. "The way you look at me," he said. "Like I'm your knight in shining armor."

"You are," she said. "You saved me, after all."

Matteo looked around one more time, at all of the people in his life. People that he loved. "No, Alessia. You saved me."

* * * * *

*Read on for an exclusive interview
with Maisey Yates!*

BEHIND THE SCENES OF
SICILY'S CORRETTI DYNASTY

It's such a huge world to create—an entire Sicilian dynasty. Did you discuss parts of it with the other writers?

Yes, we had a loop set up for discussion, and there were a *lot* of details to work out. And every so often messages would come in with the funniest subject lines I've ever seen.

How does being part of a continuity differ from when you are writing your own stories?

I think it takes a little bit to attach to characters you didn't create from scratch, but in the end, for me, I work so hard to find that attachment that I think continuity characters end up being my favorite.

What was the biggest challenge? And what did you most enjoy about it?

I think getting to the heart of my hero. Just because you've been given an outline with characters doesn't mean you've been given all the answers. In Matteo's case he was hiding something very dark and it was up to me to dig it out of him. I love a tortured hero, so this was right up my alley.

As you wrote your hero and heroine was there anything about them that surprised you?

Hee, hee... This goes with the above. Yes, Matteo surprised me with the depth of the darkness in him. I think Alessia surprised me with her strength. Every time she opened her mouth she had something sassy to say.

What was your favorite part of creating the world of Sicily's most famous dynasty?

I loved the family villas, the idea of old-world history and beauty. I love a country setting.

If you could have given your heroine one piece of advice before the opening pages of the book, what would it be?

It's never too late to try to claim your own independence... but next time maybe do it before you're walking down the aisle.

What was your hero's biggest secret?

Oh, now, see, I can't tell you that. I'd have to kill you. He's a very good dancer, though.

What does your hero love most about your heroine?

Her strength, her ability to love and feel in spite of everything she'd been through. He feels like he's on the outside, looking in at all that light and beauty, unable to touch it.

What does your heroine love most about your hero?

The man beneath the cold exterior. The man who has braved so much pain and come out the other side standing strong. The man who gave so much to free his family from their father.

Which of the Correttis would you most like to meet and why?

Matteo. Because he's a sexy beast. I can't lie.

Mills & Boon® Hardback
December 2013

ROMANCE

Defiant in the Desert	Sharon Kendrick
Not Just the Boss's Plaything	Caitlin Crews
Rumours on the Red Carpet	Carole Mortimer
The Change in Di Navarra's Plan	Lynn Raye Harris
The Prince She Never Knew	Kate Hewitt
His Ultimate Prize	Maya Blake
More than a Convenient Marriage?	Dani Collins
A Hunger for the Forbidden	Maisey Yates
The Reunion Lie	Lucy King
The Most Expensive Night of Her Life	Amy Andrews
Second Chance with Her Soldier	Barbara Hannay
Snowed in with the Billionaire	Caroline Anderson
Christmas at the Castle	Marion Lennox
Snowflakes and Silver Linings	Cara Colter
Beware of the Boss	Leah Ashton
Too Much of a Good Thing?	Joss Wood
After the Christmas Party...	Janice Lynn
Date with a Surgeon Prince	Meredith Webber

MEDICAL

From Venice with Love	Alison Roberts
Christmas with Her Ex	Fiona McArthur
Her Mistletoe Wish	Lucy Clark
Once Upon a Christmas Night...	Annie Claydon

Mills & Boon® Large Print

December 2013

ROMANCE

The Billionaire's Trophy	Lynne Graham
Prince of Secrets	Lucy Monroe
A Royal Without Rules	Caitlin Crews
A Deal with Di Capua	Cathy Williams
Imprisoned by a Vow	Annie West
Duty at What Cost?	Michelle Conder
The Rings That Bind	Michelle Smart
A Marriage Made in Italy	Rebecca Winters
Miracle in Bellaroo Creek	Barbara Hannay
The Courage To Say Yes	Barbara Wallace
Last-Minute Bridesmaid	Nina Harrington

HISTORICAL

Not Just a Governess	Carole Mortimer
A Lady Dares	Bronwyn Scott
Bought for Revenge	Sarah Mallory
To Sin with a Viking	Michelle Willingham
The Black Sheep's Return	Elizabeth Beacon

MEDICAL

NYC Angels: Making the Surgeon Smile	Lynne Marshall
NYC Angels: An Explosive Reunion	Alison Roberts
The Secret in His Heart	Caroline Anderson
The ER's Newest Dad	Janice Lynn
One Night She Would Never Forget	Amy Andrews
When the Cameras Stop Rolling...	Connie Cox

ROMANCE

The Dimitrakos Proposition	Lynne Graham
His Temporary Mistress	Cathy Williams
A Man Without Mercy	Miranda Lee
The Flaw in His Diamond	Susan Stephens
Forged in the Desert Heat	Maisey Yates
The Tycoon's Delicious Distraction	Maggie Cox
A Deal with Benefits	Susanna Carr
The Most Expensive Lie of All	Michelle Conder
The Dance Off	Ally Blake
Confessions of a Bad Bridesmaid	Jennifer Rae
The Greek's Tiny Miracle	Rebecca Winters
The Man Behind the Mask	Barbara Wallace
English Girl in New York	Scarlet Wilson
The Final Falcon Says I Do	Lucy Gordon
Mr (Not Quite) Perfect	Jessica Hart
After the Party	Jackie Braun
Her Hard to Resist Husband	Tina Beckett
Mr Right All Along	Jennifer Taylor

MEDICAL

The Rebel Doc Who Stole Her Heart	Susan Carlisle
From Duty to Daddy	Sue MacKay
Changed by His Son's Smile	Robin Gianna
Her Miracle Twins	Margaret Barker

Mills & Boon® Large Print

January 2014

ROMANCE

Challenging Dante — Lynne Graham
Captivated by Her Innocence — Kim Lawrence
Lost to the Desert Warrior — Sarah Morgan
His Unexpected Legacy — Chantelle Shaw
Never Say No to a Caffarelli — Melanie Milburne
His Ring Is Not Enough — Maisey Yates
A Reputation to Uphold — Victoria Parker
Bound by a Baby — Kate Hardy
In the Line of Duty — Ami Weaver
Patchwork Family in the Outback — Soraya Lane
The Rebound Guy — Fiona Harper

HISTORICAL

Mistress at Midnight — Sophia James
The Runaway Countess — Amanda McCabe
In the Commodore's Hands — Mary Nichols
Promised to the Crusader — Anne Herries
Beauty and the Baron — Deborah Hale

MEDICAL

Dr Dark and Far-Too Delicious — Carol Marinelli
Secrets of a Career Girl — Carol Marinelli
The Gift of a Child — Sue MacKay
How to Resist a Heartbreaker — Louisa George
A Date with the Ice Princess — Kate Hardy
The Rebel Who Loved Her — Jennifer Taylor

1213 GEN STD LP